Some Other Books by the Same Author

Cayuse Courage
Go Up the Road
(A Margaret K. McElderry Book)
The Year of Small Shadow

Rattlesnake Cave

Rattlesnake Cave

Evelyn Sibley Lampman

Illustrated by Pamela Johnson

A Margaret K. McElderry Book

Atheneum 1974 New York

Rattlesnake Cave

Chapter One

AS HE SHUFFLED HIS WAY RELUCTANTLY DOWN THE landing ramp at the Billings airport, Jamie hoped these strange relatives would like him. He really hadn't wanted to come to Montana in the first place, but both Dad and the doctor claimed it would be the best thing in the world for him.

He knew he wouldn't be making a very good first impression. There hadn't been room in his two suitcases for his books, so he carried them in a large brown paper bag. Somehow he had spilled his Coke, and the wet bag had collapsed. Now the books were stacked one on top of the other in his arms, and to keep them from falling he had to hold his chin tightly wedged against the top volume. He couldn't see where he was walking, but by keeping his eyes on the back of the man ahead, he was managing very well.

The plane had not been full, and there did not seem to be many people meeting it. Jamie did not dare turn his head or the books would fall. He stood motionless at the end of the ramp, only moving his eyes from side to side, waiting like a piece of baggage to be claimed.

"Jamie?" said a woman's voice. "Is that you?"

"Yes," he agreed, and carefully turned his whole body so there would be no accident to the books.

He hadn't seen Aunt Nora since he was a little boy, but he had seen snapshots, and he recognized her immediately. She was short, a little plump, and there were crinkles about her brown eyes. Her hair was tousled by the wind, and she wore a rather grubby yellow sweater, tan slacks and canvas shoes.

"My goodness, Jamie. You look like a walking library. Why didn't you check those books or carry them in a bag?" To his relief she didn't sound critical. Instead she seemed to think it amusing.

"I had them in a sack. But it broke," he explained.

"Well, we'd better get them to the jeep before we collect your baggage." She slid the top half of the stack into her own arms, and Jamie breathed more easily. He was beginning to get a crick in the back of his neck.

"I'm parked over here." She spoke over her shoulder, and he hurried to catch up with her. "How are your mother and father?"

"They're fine. They'll drive down to get me when Dad has his vacation," Jamie told her. For a moment he felt a little homesick. Dad's vacation wasn't until the end of August, and this was only May. Four whole months away. He wondered if Mother would cry the whole time he was gone. He remembered her as he had last seen her at the airport, dabbing at her swollen eyes with a wad of tissue. She had cried, too, the day Dad had returned from that conference with the doctor and had said that what Jamie needed was clean air and a change of environment. He was to be pulled out of school and sent to Montana to stay with Aunt Nora. It wasn't normal for any boy to sit indoors or on the patio day after day with his nose in a book. Jamie had felt like asking what else there was to do when the other kids thought you were odd and didn't ask you to play with them. But he had kept quiet. If he had admitted that, both Mother and Dad would have felt bad. They thought he preferred his own society.

"And how are you feeling?" continued Aunt Nora. "You look a little pale. But I suppose that was the flu."

"I feel fine," said Jamie. It was partly true. He was entirely recovered from the last bout of flu—he had come down with it four times last winter—but he was scared. It wasn't easy to be thrown into a family of strangers who probably wouldn't like him.

"Good." To his surprise, Aunt Nora accepted his statement without question. She wasn't going to be like Mother, always fussing that he might be covering up some hidden pain. Not that it wasn't nice to have someone worry when you didn't eat all your dinner. Or be willing to drop everything to drive you to the library when you had finished your last book.

"What in the world are all these books, anyway?" Aunt Nora looked down, reading the top title. "*A Field Guide to Western Reptiles and Amphibians.* Are you studying to be a scientist, Jamie?"

"I'm not sure what I'm going to be yet. But I thought that would be a good book to have. I understand there are lots of rattlesnakes in Montana."

"We have a few," she admitted. "But I don't think you'll be in any danger, unless you take to wandering around alone at night."

"Oh, I wouldn't do that," he assured her quickly. "I brought a book on Montana and one on Wyoming, since it's so close. I've never been there, either. I think it's a good idea to read up on a place before you see it."

"Maybe it is," said Aunt Nora. "I never thought of it."

"And I've got a couple on Custer. I looked on a map, and his battlefield's close to your ranch." He felt that an explanation was important. Carrying too many books around had once caused him trouble, and he wouldn't want Aunt Nora to think he was odd. "I guess the rest are school books. I have to finish this term's work and mail it in."

When they came to the parking lot, Aunt Nora stopped at a jeep so covered with dust that it was almost impossible to see the green paint beneath.

6

"We can leave your books in the back while we go for your bags. They'll be perfectly safe," she assured him, dumping her load on the floor. As she did so, a title caught her eye. "*Horsemanship and How to Attain It*," she read aloud. For a moment she looked startled, then her eyes began to twinkle.

"I forgot about that one," admitted Jamie. He could tell she was trying not to laugh, and he felt his face grow warm. "I thought it might be useful."

"I'm sure it will," said Aunt Nora. "Now let's go see about your baggage."

As he followed her back to the building, Jamie told himself that Aunt Nora was like all the others. She couldn't understand that it was perfectly natural to want to learn all about the strange, exciting things that made up the world. Reading about them was the only way he could do it. Adults didn't have time to answer questions. Usually they told him to look it up and he'd remember it longer, which was another way of saying they didn't know themselves. So a year or so ago Jamie had fallen into the habit of carrying around a couple of books to read in his spare time.

Obviously it wasn't the thing to do. The kids at school made jokes about it. Some of them asked if he was trying to impress the teachers. And before he knew it, everyone was calling him Genius. He had never had many friends, but after that even those few began avoiding him.

It was no fun being an outsider, so Jamie left the books at home. Sometimes he even pretended not to know the answer when the teacher called on him. No one seemed to notice. Everything remained the same.

And now Aunt Nora thought his stack of books amusing. He wished he hadn't brought so many.

Once the luggage was collected and the jeep headed out on the paved highway, Aunt Nora redeemed herself.

"There's a Montana map in the glove compartment if you'd like to see where we're going," she told him.

Jamie loved maps, although he seldom had a chance to follow a highway on one. He took it out eagerly, and she jabbed with her finger to show the location of the Bennett ranch.

"Why, it's next to an Indian reservation! The Northern Cheyenne," he exclaimed in delight. "I should have got a book—" He stopped short in the middle of the sentence. Aunt Nora thought he'd brought too many books already.

"Never mind," she said gaily. "We'll drive over to the Custer Monument some day, and you can buy one there. They have lots of books on Indians."

"The Custer battlefield is on another reservation. The Crow," he said, studying the map carefully. "It's right next to the Cheyenne. It's nice that they can be together."

"It's all right now." Aunt Nora speeded up to pass a heavily loaded camper. "In the beginning, I'm not so sure. The Crows and the Cheyenne were enemies then. I don't think the government was too particular about where they placed the tribes, so long as they were out of the way."

"But we go right through both of them." Jamie was pleased. It was a long way to the spot on the map that Aunt Nora had pointed out as the ranch, and the red highway line ran straight through the middle of the two reservations.

"Not today. We only skirt a corner of the Crow reservation. Then we'll strike out on a dirt road that isn't marked. It's too far to go around today. But don't worry," she added, seeing the disappointment on his face. "You'll see plenty of Indians. We even have one working for us, Charley White."

Jamie finally gave up studying the map and began looking at the country whizzing by. It was very different from his own closely populated section of southern California. Here were miles and miles of rangeland, most of it fenced along the highway, with black cattle grazing on the spring grass. Sometimes there were a few antelope or deer mingled with the herds. Like the cattle, they did not even bother to look up at the sound of the passing cars.

There were glimpses of occasional farm buildings, approached by long dirt roads, and once they slowed up for a small town. They crossed a racing stream, swollen with melting mountain snow, which he was able to identify as the Bighorn River. Although he hadn't yet read his books on Custer, he knew it was historic ground.

"Now we're on the Crow reservation," announced

Aunt Nora finally. "The highway runs through the corner a little way."

Jamie stared out the window. The land looked the same as before, untilled fields, rough and broken with arroyos, with the faint green fuzz of May growth. There was not an Indian in sight.

Shortly after that Aunt Nora turned off the main highway onto a side road. Once someone must have poured gravel on it, but most of the rocks had sunk into the ground. Now the mud had dried to powder, and the jeep bounced in and out of chuckholes, raising a great cloud of dust.

"Hold on," said Aunt Nora jerkily. "We've got about thirty miles of this, but it's still the shortest way home."

Jamie clutched the seat and wondered how she could be so cheerful. He had never traveled so rough a road, and with the rising dust he could only see straight ahead. Both sides were obscured. Mother would be upset if she knew he was breathing all this dust. She would say it was hard on his lungs. He was glad she didn't know.

Aunt Nora drove doggedly, holding tight to the wheel without speaking, and Jamie stopped talking, too. Once he got over the initial shock, he rather enjoyed the experience. This must be the way the pioneers in the covered wagons had felt, he decided, only with many oxen stirring up the dust ahead it would be even denser.

After what seemed like a very long time, they

arrived at a graveled section, and Aunt Nora gave a sigh of relief.

"We're almost home," she told him. "This is the beginning of our land. Bill had some gravel spread this month."

When the dust settled, Jamie could see the fence lines. One enclosed a large field containing a crop that Aunt Nora identified as oats. Another was pasturage, with the inevitable herd of black cattle. Then the road curved to skirt a cluster of tall rocks, which rose out of the surrounding ground like a brown stone castle.

"Funny rocks," said Jamie in surprise.

"Those are our Indian rocks," Aunt Nora told him. "There are caves in the other side with pictures in them."

"You mean Indian pictographs?"

"Yes." She seemed surprised that he knew the word. "They're very old. Sometimes people drive up to see them. We don't mind. Our hired-man's grandfather spends his summers there, waiting for tourists. They pay him a little something to let them take his picture."

"Are the pictographs Cheyenne or Crow?" Jamie was far more interested in the picture writing than in a modern Indian who made his living from tourists.

"Probably older than either," said Aunt Nora. "Although the Cheyenne claim them. Once a year they hold a powwow there, but I think it's just to please White Fang, Charley's grandfather. He's very old and a bit senile, but the tribe is good to him. They humor him in his little ways. Charley drops him off at the rocks on his way to work each morning and picks him up at night."

"I'd like to see the caves," said Jamie. He wished he had known about them before so he could have found a book on Indian pictographs.

"You will," Aunt Nora told him positively. "It's only a mile from the ranch house. You can walk it easily."

Jamie looked at her in surprise. His mother always drove him six blocks back and forth to the library. But with Aunt Nora's next remark, he forgot all about that.

"You'd better read your book about reptiles first," she added, smiling a little. "The rocks are crawling with rattlesnakes."

Chapter Two

"HEY, WAKE UP. ARE YOU GOING TO SLEEP ALL DAY? Mom says breakfast's on the table."

Jamie opened blurred eyes and found his cousin Dick standing over him.

"What time is it?" he asked weakly. It seemed to him he had barely gone to sleep.

"Six o'clock," said Dick. "We let you sleep in since it's your first day."

He left and Jamie struggled out of bed. Six o'clock! Usually he was still asleep at that hour. Living on a ranch was going to be very different. He wished now that he hadn't read so late last night. Everyone else had gone to bed at nine, but it had been nearly twelve by the time he turned off his own light.

They were all sitting at a table in the center of the kitchen when he arrived, and Aunt Nora had just put down a platter of pancakes, fresh from the stove.

"Long plane trip kind of tire you out?" asked Uncle Bill genially. He was a broad-shouldered, good-natured man with weathered skin and hair that was turning gray above his ears.

Jamie nodded guiltily and looked down at his plate. It already contained two fried eggs and a slice of ham, and now Aunt Nora was passing him the pancake platter. He could never eat that much food. He would have preferred juice and dry cereal, but he didn't like to ask for substitutions the first day.

"I don't see how riding on a plane could tire anybody," objected Dick. "All you do is sit."

Dick was eighteen, and Jamie had already decided they didn't have much in common. His cousin was wrapped up in his own affairs, his graduation from high school in a few weeks, a new horse that he was trying to break, and whether or not he would be permitted the use of the family car on Saturday night.

"You ever ridden on a plane, Dick?" asked Charley White, and when Dick grinned and shook his head, he added, "Then how do you know it wouldn't tire you out?"

Jamie hadn't been able to figure out Charley White. He worked for Uncle Bill and took his meals with the family, but he didn't sleep there. Every night he drove to his home on the Cheyenne reservation in a rusty old car, returning early the next morning.

It was the first time Jamie had been in such close

contact with an Indian, and he was a little disappointed. Charley didn't live up to the image he had formed from watching TV Westerns. True, his skin was bronze and his hair was black, but it was cut short, much shorter than Dick's. And his face wasn't stern and expressionless as Jamie had always heard Indians were taught to keep their faces. He laughed a lot and made jokes, and he was very considerate of Aunt Nora, even though Indians were not supposed to have a high regard for women. When Uncle Bill had asked him about a new treatment for some cattle disease that was being used at the university, Charley had gone into a long, technical explanation. He was in his third year at Bozeman but had run out of money, so he was staying out this term to make enough to return.

"You want to move that herd today, Mr. Bennett?" Charley changed the subject when Dick only grinned and refused to argue about plane travel. "Grass is getting a little short in that pasture."

"I'd planned to," said Uncle Bill. "But it will take two of us, and Diamond's about ready to foal. Somebody should stay with her."

"I could skip school," offered Dick. "I wouldn't miss much this late in the year."

"You'll not skip school," declared his mother firmly. "Not if I have to help your dad move the herd myself. I think Charley should stay with Diamond. He's so good with her."

Charley said he'd do whatever they wanted, then

15

he announced that as he had driven by that morning he had seen a dead lamb in one of the fields. He had stopped to investigate, and there had been a coyote at work. Somebody had better get it before it wiped out the flock.

"Do you have cows and sheep both?" Jamie looked up from his plate in surprise. "I thought cattlemen and sheepmen hated each other."

"You've been looking at too many movies," accused Dick, and Jamie blushed.

"I guess it used to be that way," said Uncle Bill. "Nowdays a rancher has to have a lot of fingers in the pot just to keep going." He looked at Charley, and his eyes sparkled. "I think those cows will be all right for another day. We'll move the herd tomorrow. You stay and keep an eye on Diamond, Charley, in case she needs help. There's a couple of bridles that need mending, too."

"I suppose you're going after that coyote," said Dick enviously. "Bet you don't get him."

"I'll be glad to go, Mr. Bennett," offered Charley slyly. "The Cheyenne are great trackers, you know."

"So is Butch," declared Uncle Bill. "He needs a workout anyway. Butch and I will bring him in."

"Butch never smelled out a coyote in his life," said Dick. "What we need around here is a hound. If you'd just let me skip school—"

"No chance," said his father. He looked at Jamie and smiled. "How about you? Want to go with me this morning and kill yourself a coyote?"

"Oh, no," said Jamie, shuddering at the idea. "I couldn't kill a coyote. I wouldn't even want to see it done."

The smile faded from Uncle Bill's face, and Dick's gasp of disbelief was plainly audible.

"He's only just arrived," Aunt Nora reminded them quickly. "Jamie has no idea of the damage a coyote can do to a rancher. He'll learn."

"I guess so," said Uncle Bill. He took a last drink of coffee and stood up. "Well, we can't sit around here all day."

As he pushed back his chair, Charley White looked at Jamie. Now his face was expressionless, as an Indian's should be.

"You'll have to meet my grandfather," he said. "White Fang wouldn't kill a coyote either."

When the others left, Jamie sat in his chair, poking at his unfinished breakfast. If only he'd kept quiet. Twice in one meal he had made comments that had laid him open to criticism. Uncle Bill had been pleasant about his stupid question about sheep and cattle on the same ranch, but there had been no mistaking the scorn on Dick's face. Even worse was Jamie's refusal to hunt a coyote. None of them understood that. They all wanted to go. Perhaps, on a ranch, where livestock were at stake, it was a necessity, but they also seemed to look on it as a sport. Why couldn't he have just begged off because of schoolwork? They would have understood that. Now his impulsive remarks had lost him their respect. They would never like him again.

Aunt Nora gathered up the dirty dishes, then poured herself another cup of coffee.

"Finish your breakfast, Jamie," she advised. "This morning you're going to start on your chores."

"Chores?" He stared at her in surprise. At home all he had to do was make sure his soiled clothes were put in the laundry basket. Then he remembered. Dad wanted Aunt Nora to put him to work in order to toughen him up. Mother had cried even harder than before when she heard that.

"Everybody works on a ranch," she told him, smiling. "And I've got just the job for you. Feeding the bummers twice a day."

"Bummers?"

"Some are orphans and some have been rejected by their mothers," she explained. "Don't ask me why. We have four lambs and a bull calf that have to be bottle-fed morning and evenings. I've been doing it, but if you'll take over the job it will save me a lot of work."

Jamie nodded eagerly. This was something he'd enjoy. It wasn't taking the life of an animal. It was giving life. He wondered why a mother sheep would reject one of her own offspring and wished he had brought more books. He doubted if he could find the answer in any of those that stood in a neat row in his room.

Aunt Nora had the gruel already mixed in a bucket. She showed Jamie how to funnel it into a large Coke bottle and fasten a rubber nipple over the end. Then they went to the barnyard behind the house. As soon as they reached the wire fence they were besieged by white lambs, each bumping and pushing for the first turn at the bottle. A black Angus calf tried to squeeze in, but the lambs formed a wriggling wedge and would not let him through.

"Do we have to feed them through the fence?" Jamie was surprised that Aunt Nora had not entered the barnyard.

"And have them slopping over the bucket?" Aunt Nora thrust the filled bottle through the wires and the nipple was seized by one of the lambs. The others stood by, bumping each other and bleating, but they did not have long to wait. In no time at all the bottle was empty. It must have been enough to fill his stomach, for the lamb romped off, happy and satisfied.

Jamie refilled the bottle, and another lamb seized the nipple ahead of the others. This time he felt a little surer of himself, and with his left hand he groped through the wires to pet the feeding animal. It did not feel soft and fleecy as he had imagined lambs would be. The white curly hair grew thinly over a bony head, and he could feel two bumps where someday horns would appear.

Charley White came to the barn door while they were there and waved to them.

"Anything yet?" shouted Aunt Nora, and Charley shook his head.

When they finished, Aunt Nora said that next time Jamie wouldn't need her. He could take over the whole thing himself. It would be a great help, because she had plenty to do without mixing food and holding bottles twice a day. Jamie felt proud that he could do something to please her.

"Better do your schoolwork now," she advised, and he obediently went to his room.

The principal at home had agreed that it would be foolish for Jamie to transfer to a Montana school so late in the year. Since he was an exceptional student, he could work on his own, mail in the assignments, and be promoted with the rest of the class.

He found pencil and paper and opened his math book to the proper page. That was as far as he got. Instead of the problem to be solved he kept remembering his mistakes at the breakfast table. They weighed like a heavy load inside him and made work impossible.

Wherever he went, things went wrong. He wasn't like other boys, and nobody liked him. Except Mother. But mothers always liked their children. They were supposed to.

Usually fathers did, too, but sometimes Jamie wondered about his dad. They didn't see each other too often. Dad's job required lots of traveling, and even when he was home, he and Jamie didn't have much in common. Dad played golf with his friends on the weekends, and he never missed a football game on TV. Once he suggested that Jamie watch with him, but after the first five minutes Jamie excused himself and went to his room to read. He was never invited to watch again. Dad was proud of the straight A's on Jamie's report card and said so. But after the congratulations were over, they seemed to have trouble finding something to talk about.

In his own way, Dad was probably fond of him. He was always concerned when he came home and found Jamie sick in bed. After the last bout of flu, he had insisted on talking to the doctor himself. When he came home, his mind was made up.

"What Jamie needs is to get out of here for awhile," he said, and his voice was very firm. "The doctor says fresh air, exercise, and a change of environment. I'll call Nora. A few months on a ranch will do him good."

"Oh, no, Bob." Mother's face grew fearful. "Jamie's delicate. I'm not saying anything against your sister. But Nora won't understand a boy like Jamie."

"She'll understand," said Dad grimly.

"Then I'll go with him," offered Mother. "You can get along without me for a couple of months, but Jamie will need me."

"No, he won't." Jamie had never heard his father's voice so determined. "He's a big boy now. Almost twelve. He's to go alone. And it will be four months, not two. We'll drive up and get him when I have my vacation."

At that point Mother had begun crying, but Dad had not relented. Jamie had never seen him so determined about anything. Always before, decisions about Jamie had been left up to Mother. This time Dad had made the decision, and he was sticking to it.

For the first time in his life, Jamie found that he was unable to concentrate on his lessons. He closed the book and went downstairs.

Aunt Nora was kneading bread dough, her floured hands moving deftly.

"Finished already?" she asked.

"I'll help you with that," offered Jamie, ignoring her question. It would be nice to win her praise again. "It doesn't look hard."

"It's harder than you think." She laughed. "There's a trick to it. Why don't you go out and stretch your legs a little? Or go down to the barn and talk to Charley."

He felt like a balloon that was slowly losing air. Aunt Nora had seemed genuinely pleased that he was going to take over feeding the baby animals. But now she didn't want him around. She was brushing him off.

He went outside onto the back porch. Zeke, the fuzzy black and white puppy that Uncle Bill, with the help of Butch, planned to train to be a second sheep dog, greeted him enthusiastically. Jamie picked him up, and Zeke squirmed with delight, licking his face with a rough, red tongue.

"At least you like me," Jamie said to the dog. "You don't think I'm odd."

For a moment he considered going to the barn to

talk with Charley White. But Charley would be busy. Maybe he wouldn't want company, especially the company of someone who didn't want to watch the killing of a coyote. Maybe it would be better to do a little exploring on his own.

It was a beautiful day. Overhead the sky was blue, with just a few white clouds floating above the mountains in the west. In the east the land went on and on, climbing the slopes of pasture, studded with small trees and bushes. If he walked that way he might get lost, and he wouldn't want that to happen.

The road over which they had driven yesterday ran west. It seemed to disappear in the range of mountains that supported the sky. Closer at hand was the great jagged pile of rocks containing the Indian pictographs. Aunt Nora said they were a mile away, but in the clear, sparkling air they looked much closer. Maybe she was mistaken about the distance. Of course, there were rattlesnakes there, but if he was very careful where he stepped, he shouldn't have any trouble, and it was someplace to go. He set out immediately down the road for the Indian rocks.

Chapter Three

RUBBER-SOLED TENNIS SHOES WERE NOT MEANT FOR walking on graveled roads, and it took longer than Jamie expected to reach the rocks. He was afraid to step off the road itself and use the narrow strips beside the wire fences, because snakes might be hiding in the grass or bushes. Until he read the book on reptiles, he couldn't be sure about the habits of rattlesnakes. They could be lurking anywhere, ready to coil and strike.

The clear air had been deceptive, and now Jamie decided it must be even more than a mile to the rocks. He didn't think he had ever walked so far before. The muscles in the back of his legs were getting stiff, and he would have liked to sit down and catch his breath. There was no place to sit except the road itself, so he continued doggedly on.

The sun was well up by the time he reached the beginning of the great mass of stones. They were like the short spur of a mountain chain, longer than he had perceived from the car, and even taller than he had imagined. They reared upward from the rough ground well over a hundred feet, like a giant eruption on the face of the landscape. It was too bad he hadn't included a book on geology, he told himself, wondering how this phenomenon had come about.

This section was not fenced, so he stepped cautiously off the graveled road, grateful to be rid of the sharp stones but scanning the ground before he placed each foot. As he circled the rocks, he could see that they curved inward at each side, leaving an open space fifty or sixty feet across.

It was like being in a great unceilinged room, with tall rock walls that stretched up and up on three sides, so he had to tilt his head to see the sky. Two of the walls sloped upward gently, and their rough faces were broken and jagged, with occasional sturdy bushes or plants growing in the crevices. Since the ground below was strewn with large and small boulders, Jamie concluded that pieces of the rock must have been broken off by winter storms.

The third cliff, however, looked smooth and precipitous. Nothing grew on its surface, nor did it seem to have suffered much damage from the elements. High up on its face, seventy or eighty feet from the ground, he could see a round black hole that must be the entrance to a cave. If this was the one containing the Indian pictographs, he would never see them, he told himself. He could never climb that sheer cliff. Perhaps a professional mountain climber might, but Jamie had never been very good in sports.

"You bring camera?" demanded a voice a little to one side of him. "One picture, one dollar."

Jamie jumped. He had thought he was alone. Now he saw that a very old Indian was sitting on the ground nearby, his back propped against a boulder. He wore a pair of faded Levi's and a gray work shirt, with a red bandanna tied around his neck. On his head was a curiously shaped hat, made of skins, open at the top so that the center parting of his gray hair was fully visible. The hat was tied under his chin with thongs, and the face beneath was so crossed with wrinkles that Jamie thought instinctively of a dried-up apple.

For a moment he was frightened, then he remembered Aunt Nora had said that Charley White's grandfather spent his days at the cave, waiting for tourists.

"Hello," he said. "You must be Mr. White Fang. I'm Jamie Steele. Mr. and Mrs. Bennett are my uncle and aunt. I've come to spend the summer with them. And I know your grandson, Charley."

"No camera?" asked the old man suspiciously. "No picture?"

"No, I don't have a camera. I wanted to see the

pictographs—the pictures the Indians made in the cave. Are they in that one up there? How do you get up the cliff?"

"Not there," objected White Fang quickly. "No man climb there. Too dangerous. That cave filled with rattlesnakes. Rattlesnakes live there always."

"Really?" Jamie stared at the sheer cliff stretching upward toward the sky. Just below the opening he could see two thin, almost vertical, lines that seemed to be worn away in the surface. "Do they always stay there? What do they live on? How did they get up there in the first place?"

White Fang ignored his questions. With a dirty thumb he pointed to the sloping cliff on the opposite side.

"Picture cave there," he announced. "Take trail. See pictures made by old ones."

"Thank you," said Jamie. Then he hesitated. "Will I run into rattlesnakes there, too?"

White Fang shrugged.

"You watch," he advised. "Open ears for buzz."

If he had been alone, Jamie might not have ventured up an unknown trail. However, he didn't want to admit his fear to this old man. White Fang was an Indian, and Indians were always fearless. Cautious, yes, but they scorned anyone who was lacking in bravery. All the books and movies said so.

He started in the direction White Fang had indicated, stepping carefully and listening for rattles. Soon he found a well-marked trail. It was steep and led around crags and boulders, but there were occasional bushes he could grasp to give him a hand, and a few level spots where he could pause to get his breath.

When he reached the first of them, he sat down. He had wanted to rest before, as soon as he reached the rocks, but he had been shy about admitting this to White Fang. He sat on a boulder and pretended to be examining the rocks. The Indian, he was glad to see, was not watching; he was still sitting in the sun, staring straight ahead. Jamie massaged the muscles in his legs for a long time. Then he stood up wearily and began climbing again.

He rested several times on the ascent, partly because of his legs and partly from lack of breath. He had not known that climbing a cliff made anyone pant so much.

Finally he reached the cave. It was not nearly so high in the cliff as the one that sheltered the rattlesnakes, nor was it dark. The opening was wide enough so there was plenty of light to see the writing.

The first thing that met his eyes was an inscription, written with chalk. "Gary loves Sheila." Farther on he read a blurred "Kilroy was here." There were other English phrases, some in chalk, a few scratched with rock on the stony surface, and as he read them Jamie felt a great surge of disappointment. This was no pictograph cave. It was just some place for idiots to leave their handiwork. Then he looked at the walls more closely.

The pictographs were there. They had been done in red clay, now faded and indistinct. There was the drawing of some animal, perhaps a deer, and surely that was the sun and a mountain. The modern chalk writings had been deliberately smeared over the older pictures, making them hard to see.

For a long time he stayed there, trying to figure them out. Uncle Bill should be told, he decided. If he knew that tourists were deliberately marring the ancient pictographs perhaps he would close the caves to the public. People who had no more consideration than this shouldn't be allowed to come.

When he finally came down, White Fang was still sitting in the same position on the ground. After a moment, Jamie sat down beside him. When the old Indian made no objections to his being there, he stretched out his legs gratefully.

"I saw them," he announced. "The pictures are still there. I didn't know what most of them meant."

"Only old ones knew," said White Fang. "Pictures sacred."

"You haven't seen them for a long time?" asked Jamie cautiously. He was relieved when the old man shook his head. White Fang wouldn't like to have the pictures marred.

The old Indian did not seem to want to talk, and for some reason Jamie didn't either. It was pleasant to sit in the sun, looking at the three stone walls. There was companionship in their silence. Once he thought of his blunders at the breakfast table, but they didn't seem so important now. He had plenty of time to prove to Dick and Uncle Bill that he had other qualities to recommend him. He didn't have to kill a coyote to be admired.

Then he remembered what Charley White had said about his grandfather and the coyotes, and he broke the long silence.

"Charley says you wouldn't kill a coyote," he said. "Neither would I."

White Fang turned his head. From beneath the folds of wrinkles, black eyes regarded him carefully.

"Kill only to eat," he said. "Never eat coyote. Only kill when medicine man need coyote skin for sacred arrows. Coyote special animal. Eat buffalo. Eat antelope, beaver, rabbit. Otter, wolf not good. If man hungry and no game, can eat wolf. Stay back from fire when cooking. Smell bad."

The words made sense to Jamie. If he were starving, he supposed he could kill game. A person would probably do anything to stay alive. He leaned back against the boulder, feeling very much at peace.

Between them on the ground was a leather jacket. Probably White Fang had worn it this morning when his grandson dropped him off at the rocks. It had been chilly before the sun was up.

Then Jamie's eye was caught by something lying on top of the jacket. It was leather, too, and the same color, so he hadn't noticed it before. It was a bag, gathered at one end, with a long rawhide strap. There was a design on one side made of beads and shells. Without thinking, he picked it up to examine it more closely.

The next moment White Fang snatched it from his hand, and the wrinkles in his face had re-formed into lines of anger.

"No touch!" The old voice cracked sharply. "No touch medicine bag of someone else."

"I'm sorry," apologized Jamie quickly. "I didn't know. I was just—"

"Go home," ordered White Fang sternly. "Leave this sacred place. Not want you here."

Jamie stumbled to his feet. There was something about the old man's face that frightened him. That was silly, of course. White Fang was too old and feeble to hurt anyone.

"I didn't mean—" he began, but White Fang would not listen.

"Go home," he ordered. "Do not come again."

Chapter Four

"GRANDFATHER'S MEDICINE BAG IS SACRED TO HIM,"
explained Charley White. "Even I wouldn't dare
handle it, except to put it in his coffin when he dies.
He didn't understand when you picked it up. I'll
explain it to him tonight. I'll tell him that you
didn't know, and when he calms down, he'll be all
right."

"I hope so," said Jamie unhappily. "I like your
grandfather. I want to be friends with him."

As soon as he returned to the ranch, he had gone
to the barn where Charley White was sitting in the
sunny doorway, mending a bridle and keeping an
eye on the mare, Diamond. He had reported the
whole story of his meeting with White Fang at the
rocks, and Charley had listened carefully.

"White Fang does not give his friendship easily."

Charley seemed to be choosing his words. "It will take a long time, but if you're really sincere—"

"Oh, I am," Jamie assured him hastily. "I wouldn't have touched that little bag for anything if I'd known he wouldn't like it. What's in it, anyway?"

"Only White Fang knows that. The man who made it, his father, has been dead for years. He was a medicine man of the Cheyenne, and he gave the bag to White Fang when he was sixteen and had his first vision. Nobody has medicine bags anymore. Probably Grandfather's is the only one left on the reservation."

"How old is your grandfather?"

"I'm not sure, but he's in his nineties." Charley pulled on the leather strap he had just mended to test its strength. "He was the youngest son, born after the battle of the Little Big Horn, and that was in 1876. He had two older brothers who fought against Custer. One of them was killed then, and the other died later. White Fang grew up on his older brother's stories, and sometimes he retells them as though they had happened to him."

"I wish he'd tell them to me," said Jamie wistfully.

"Maybe he will sometime," said Charley. He stood up and went back inside.

The big meal on the ranch was at noon, and because Jamie was hungry, he ate everything that was served to him. Uncle Bill came riding in shortly before, with Butch trailing wearily behind. They had got the coyote, he announced happily, at least *a* coyote, and he hoped it was the one that had been raiding the sheep.

To Jamie's relief, Uncle Bill seemed to have forgotten his unfortunate remarks at the breakfast table. He inquired how Jamie had occupied his time, and when he heard about the walk to the Indian rocks, he asked why he hadn't ridden one of the horses.

"I don't know how to ride." Jamie almost mentioned the book on horsemanship but thought better of it. Aunt Nora had laughed when she saw it.

"That's what comes of bringing up kids in the city," said Uncle Bill disapprovingly. "Charley, how about throwing a saddle on Old Sal and letting Jamie practice in the corral this afternoon? You can keep an eye on him, too, can't you?"

Charley agreed that he could. Diamond was slower in producing her new colt than they expected, and it was only a few steps from the barn to the corral.

"Are those your tightest pants?" Uncle Bill stared critically at Jamie's new Levi's. Because they shrank in the washing, and also to allow for summer growth, they had been purchased a little large.

"I've got an old pair that fit tighter, but they're about worn out. Mother just sent them along for extras."

"Put them on. Baggy seats in the saddle mean sore behinds afterward," said Uncle Bill. "And while you're about it, wear boots if you have any. You shouldn't be walking around in low shoes. You're

lucky you didn't run into a rattler at the rocks today."

Jamie hurried upstairs to change. The book on
horsemanship would have probably told him about
wearing tight pants. And undoubtedly the one on
reptiles would have warned about wearing boots in
snake country. As soon as he had time, he was going
to have to read everything fast.

His legs were still stiff from his morning's walk,
but he didn't mention it. People might think he was
a sissy. And he didn't mention the long lecture
Mother had given him on horses.

"I suppose you'll have to learn to ride," she had
said fearfully. "Your father thinks it's a good idea,
and on a ranch it may be expected. But be very careful, Jamie. Make sure it's a safe animal, one that's
been ridden a lot. Whatever you do, don't try to ride
one of those wild horses that aren't used to people.
And hang on very tightly."

The mare that was saddled and waiting when he
arrived at the corral looked safe enough. But she
was anything but beautiful. Her coat was white with
dapples of gray, and the hair was long and tangled.
She stood with her head hanging, but when Charley
led Jamie to her side, she turned and regarded him
with speculative brown eyes.

"This is Old Sal," said Charley. "She's gentle as a
kitten. We always bring her out for people who've
never been around horses. Sometimes we even loan
her to neighbors when they've got visitors. Her

mouth's not as soft as most, but don't take advantage of that. She'll let you know if you do."

He showed Jamie how to put his left foot in the stirrup, grasp the stirrup leather with his right hand, then swing himself into the saddle. It was especially hard to do with sore legs, and it took several tries before he could accomplish it. Finally he slipped into the seat with one leg on each side of the horse. It seemed to Jamie that he was very far off the ground, and he grasped the reins tightly. Old Sal's ears went back, and she shook her head.

"Don't do that," warned Charley. "You don't need a death grip on those reins. Loosen up, but not too loose or she'll wander. The feel of the reins is something you'll get used to, and Old Sal will help you."

Jamie relaxed some of the tightness, but he still felt insecure. The stirrups seemed too long, and his legs dangled awkwardly.

Charley led the horse around the corral the first time, then told Jamie to try it alone.

"And don't lean back on that cantle," he ordered. "The cantle is the upright back of your saddle. It's a support for your back, but it's not to lean on. Old Sal will buck you off if you try it. Lean your weight forward."

The threat was enough. Jamie didn't want to be thrown to the ground. He leaned forward, and to his surprise he found that his feet now adjusted themselves to the stirrups.

Charley watched without further comment, and

when Jamie had circled the corral twice, he announced that he was going back to Diamond.

Old Sal continued around and around in a slow, patient walk, which, after awhile, began to get tiresome. Jamie decided it was time to go a little faster.

"Get up, Sal," he ordered. "Let's gallop!"

He clicked his tongue in the way cowboys in movies did, kicked with his feet, and took a fresh grip on the reins. The next moment he was on the ground.

It happened so fast that he hardly had time to think. He had been telling himself that riding a horse was simple. You just got on and the horse did the rest. Now he was lying in the dust, while Old Sal stood off a little way, regarding him with sad brown eyes.

He wasn't hurt, and he got to his feet, shaking a little straw from his hair and staring back at the horse. Was this a test? On TV, cowhands always gave city dudes difficult horses to ride on their first visit to a ranch. Then they hung over the fence and laughed. Old Sal didn't look like a difficult horse, but she had certainly bucked him off.

He didn't know that Uncle Bill had come up in time to witness the whole humiliating experience until he heard his voice.

"Do you know what you did wrong?"

Jamie spun around, his cheeks reddening.

"You kicked with your feet and told her to get going," explained Uncle Bill. "Then you pulled on the reins, which meant stop. Sal was trying to tell you to keep your commands straight."

It was exactly what he had done, and Jamie grinned foolishly.

"What are you going to do now?" asked Uncle Bill. "Had enough?"

"Oh, no. I'll try again," said Jamie quickly. The city dude, especially if he turned out to be the hero, always mounted a bucking horse immediately after he had been thrown.

"Good boy," said Uncle Bill approvingly. "No, no. Left side. Always mount on the left side."

Jamie corrected his mistake, and Old Sal stood patiently while he put his foot in the stirrup and finally pulled himself up.

"OK," shouted Uncle Bill. "This time loosen your reins when you tell her to go."

Maybe Old Sal didn't gallop very fast, but it seemed like it. Jamie found it exciting to feel the gentle wind in his face, to know that the big animal beneath him was obeying his bidding. After they had circled the corral three times, he brought her to a triumphant stop at the side of the fence where Uncle Bill was watching.

"This is fun," he declared happily. "Sal is a wonderful horse."

"She is that," agreed Uncle Bill solemnly. "She's taught more people to ride than I could shake a stick at. She's one of a kind, Old Sal. I think she'd better be yours while you're with us."

"Really?" Jamie leaned down and patted the rough

coat. "Do you think maybe I could brush her a little?"

"I certainly do," agreed his uncle. "First, though, I think you ought to practice mounting and dismounting. Old Sal will stand for you."

Jamie agreed that he could use a little more practice in that. Uncle Bill went to the barn to see how Diamond was getting along, and Old Sal stood while he climbed painfully in and out of the saddle. From time to time they had a few sedate gallops around the corral, but eventually Jamie decided Sal had worked long enough for one day.

"You wait here," he told her, patting her neck. "I'll get a brush and give you a nice rubdown. I'll have to get Charley to show me how to take off your saddle. I don't know where to start."

When he reached the barn, he found that Diamond had finally had her colt. Uncle Bill and Charley were standing there, grinning at each other and admiring a small animal with shaky legs that looked too long for its body. It was a bay, with a black mane and tail, and looked like an unsteady miniature of its mother.

"Look at that," cried Uncle Bill. "Isn't he a dandy?"

"Yes," agreed Jamie. But privately he decided he liked white ones best, the kind with little gray splotches.

There was no need to pretend that he wasn't sore and stiff that night. Everyone seemed to expect it.

"The first time on a horse isn't easy," said Uncle Bill. "Especially when you get thrown. You tell your dad I said you'd make a real cowpoke someday."

"The best thing is a hot soak in the tub," suggested Aunt Nora. "And I've got some liniment if you think you need it."

Jamie almost forgot his aches and pains in the warmth of their praise. For once he had done something right.

He soaked a long time in the bathtub, then went straight to bed. It was too early to go to sleep, but he felt more comfortable lying down. This would be a good time to write a letter to Mother. He had promised to write every day, but he hadn't remembered until now. He got his school tablet and a pencil, and began to write rapidly.

"Dear Mother,

I am fine. The ride on the plane was fine. I wasn't airsick. Aunt Nora was there to meet me."

He paused, wondering what to say next. Those were the things she had worried about all the way to the airport, but they made a very brief letter. He didn't think Mother would be interested in the Indian rocks or pictographs, and she would be frantic if she knew about the rattlesnakes. Then he remembered Uncle Bill's message to his father, and began writing again.

"Today I rode a horse. Her name is Sal. She is

gentle, but she bucked me off."

He stopped and carefully erased the last five words. That would really worry Mother. She'd probably take the next plane to Montana. After that he finished rapidly.

"Uncle Bill says to tell Dad I did fine and that I'll make a good cowpoke someday.

Your loving son,
Jamie"

He breathed a sigh of relief as he folded the letter. His mother seemed very far away right now, but he had done his duty. He would keep his promise and write every day. He only hoped he could find enough to say that wouldn't worry her.

He was very tired, but when he looked at his watch it was a little past seven. That was much too early to go to sleep. He decided to read some of the book about reptiles. As soon as Charley had straightened things out with his grandfather, Jamie wanted to go back to the rocks.

Chapter Five

THE NEXT MORNING CHARLEY AND UNCLE BILL SADdled horses, preparatory to moving the herd of cattle from one field to another. Dick again offered to skip school to help and was turned down. Jamie wished that he and Sal would be invited, but he wasn't surprised when they weren't.

He fed the baby animals and did two pages of math problems, then wandered out to the corral. Now that Sal was to be his horse, she wouldn't be turned out with the others. She would stay in the corral, where she was easily accessible.

She looked at him inquiringly as he walked up and accepted the carrot he had in his hand. She looked much better after yesterday's brushing. It had stripped away some of the winter's growth of protective hair, and Jamie was sure that with daily grooming he could coax a shine to the dappled coat.

"I'd like to take a ride," he told her. "But I don't know how to put on your saddle. Charley said he'd teach me, but he's too busy this morning."

It was still early, and he wondered what he could do to entertain himself until Charley returned. He could do more schoolwork or read some of his books, but neither idea appealed to him. That was funny, because at home he read all the time.

He thought about White Fang, sitting alone at the Indian rocks and wondered if Charley had explained about the medicine bag. He had said that once his grandfather understood, he wouldn't be angry anymore. Jamie decided to take a chance and headed down the road.

He was still a little stiff, but the walking was easier for he had remembered to wear boots. The book about reptiles had repeated Uncle Bill's warning: always wear high boots in snake country. It had given another warning, too, about wearing a scarf or something that could be used as a tourniquet in case of snakebite. Jamie didn't have a scarf, but he carried a large handkerchief in his pocket. He was almost at the rocks before he remembered that he didn't have a knife to slash across the fang marks. It was too late to do anything about it now, so he kept on going.

White Fang had changed his position since yesterday. Today he was sitting on the ground beneath the cliff that contained the pictographs. His eyes were fastened on the rock wall opposite, and he did not look away from the cliff to acknowledge Jamie's arrival.

"Hello, Mr. White Fang." Jamie stood awkwardly, wondering if the Indian would let him stay. "Did Charley tell you that I didn't mean anything when I picked up your medicine bag yesterday? He said he would. I'm sorry, and I'll never touch it again."

White Fang did not answer. He kept staring at the cliff, and once he made a funny little sound in his throat that was half a sigh and half a grunt. He seemed unaware that he had company, and after a few minutes Jamie sat on the ground beside him. He, too, looked at the rock wall that held the old man's interest.

At first it seemed exactly the same as yesterday, smooth, sheer stone, with the round black hole high up on its surface. Then he looked again, blinking and staring. There seemed to be slight movements along the rock, like waving pencil lines.

"What is it?" he whispered, but White Fang did not bother to answer.

The book he had read last night on reptiles came back to him. Rattlesnakes hibernated in rocky dens and remained there until the spring weather was settled. Then the dens were depopulated as the snakes scattered to summer feeding grounds. That's what must be happening right now. The rattlesnakes were leaving their cave. They were coming down to find food and water.

"Mr. White Fang!" Jamie grasped the old man's arm in terror. "We've got to get out of here. The rattlesnakes are crawling down the cliff."

White Fang shook off his hand irritably.

"They go for water," he said. "No water here."

Despite the warm sun, Jamie's skin felt cold, and he could feel the hard thumping of his heart. His instinct told him to get to his feet and run, but he could hardly leave White Fang behind. The Indian was very old. If he should be bitten by a rattlesnake, he would need help.

The book had told Jamie exactly what to do. He would have to tie his handkerchief as a tourniquet above the bite, then make two slashes in the form of a cross over each fang mark and take three vigorous sucks, each time spitting out the venom. Then he must force White Fang to lie down while he himself ran for help. Aunt Nora would surely have permanganate crystals in the house, which was what the book recommended.

"Mr. White Fang, do you have a knife?" he whispered anxiously.

The old man frowned, but nodded. Jamie breathed a sigh of relief.

He looked away from the cliff to the ground below. A huge greenish-yellow snake had just dropped from the rocks and was inching its way slowly around the curving end of the wall. It was about fifty feet away. The book said it would have large, round blotches along the back, bordered with white or yellow. Jamie stared as hard as he could, but from this distance he could not make them out. Nevertheless, he was sure it was a rattler.

"Probably a prairie rattler," he whispered. "*Crotalus viridis viridis*."

White Fang looked at him suspiciously, then returned his stare to the cliff.

By now the snake had disappeared around the curved end of the rocks, and when a second dropped to the ground and followed the same course, Jamie was able to breath more easily. White Fang was probably right. The first thing the snakes would seek, after a winter's hibernation without food, would be water. They would undoubtedly make their way to the creek before searching for rodents. He looked behind him at the cliff containing the pictographs but decided it was probably free of snakes. That cave was too shallow for protection. Snakes, with no body warmth of their own, had to find holes deep enough so the frost could not penetrate.

"Those snakes may go as far as two miles from here." Jamie no longer felt it was necessary to whisper and spoke in a normal tone. "But they'll come back next fall. They always come back to the same den to spend the winter, but nobody knows how they find it. Do you know, Mr. White Fang?"

The old Indian looked at him scornfully.

"I am Conquers White Fangs of Snakes," he said

proudly. "My medicine is strong. I know all secrets of the snake people."

"You mean, that's your whole name?" demanded Jamie in surprise. "It's not just White Fang?"

The old Indian nodded solemnly. "My father medicine man of Elk Society. Very wise. Very powerful. Elk warriors have secret helper in snakes. Carry snake sticks in dance."

He held up two short, peeled lengths of wood. They were not more than eight or ten inches long, and one had been carved so that it resembled a snake. The sides were thickly notched, and when White Fang drew the straight piece across, it gave off a curious clicking sound. Jamie would have liked to examine the carved stick more closely, but after his experience with the medicine bag, he was afraid to ask.

"That's why you know that the snakes won't come this way. That they'll go around the rocks and head for the creek. But what if one made a mistake? What if it took the wrong turn?"

White Fang shook his head. Such a thing was clearly impossible. It was not even worth discussing.

"Are you a medicine man, too, Mr. White Fang?" asked Jamie respectfully.

"Once. Long time ago," agreed White Fang. "Once White Fang stay alone four suns in medicine hut. My helper came. My father's heart was glad. I was to take his place and place of brother who died fighting Long Hair. Now my people not believe. I am holy man no more."

"But they still honor you." Jamie wished he could do something to make the old man feel better. He had never seen anyone look so sad. "Charley's very proud of you. I can tell by the way he talks. And he brings you here to the rocks every day and takes you home at night. If he didn't think a lot of you, he wouldn't do that."

White Fang refused to be cheered up. He continued to look at the rocks, his face as mournful as before.

"How do the snakes know how to find their way back to the rocks?" asked Jamie. "The book says they always come to the same cave in the fall. How can they find their way? Of course, they could always follow the leader," he added thoughtfully. "And if they have a smell, the others might be able to follow the scent. But what if the leader got killed? Who would lead them back?"

"*Wakan Tanka*," said White Fang positively.

"Who is *Wakan Tanka?*" asked Jamie.

"*Wakan Tanka,* the Great Mystery," explained White Fang. Suddenly he pointed with one finger to an exceptionally large snake that had just dropped to the ground. "That one very old. Maybe die in summer."

"You don't mean that snake is *Wakan Tanka?*" asked Jamie in bewilderment.

When White Fang's lips made a little puffing

sound of disgust, he realized that the sentences did not go together. *Wakan Tanka,* the Great Mystery, was one thing. The observation about the big snake had nothing to do with it. Probably White Fang was changing the subject deliberately.

"They say that deer sometimes kill rattlesnakes," Jamie said, returning to the information in the book. "They jump on them with their hooves and get away before the snake can strike. Did you ever see that happen, Mr. White Fang?"

White Fang nodded solemnly. Yes, it was so. He had seen it happen.

"And it isn't true that prairie dogs and owls live in the same hole with rattlesnakes, the way the early settlers used to claim?"

White Fang permitted himself a scornful laugh at the absurdity.

"Do you know that today there are rattlesnake farms? Men milk them to get the poison." Jamie decided to try one of the modern scientific facts he had read.

"Men?" White Fang laughed again. "That woman's work. When my father need poison from snake, my mother got it. Take no special words."

Jamie gave up trying to impress him with the information he had found in the book. White Fang seemed to know all about it. They sat companionably watching the snakes descend the cliff.

As Jamie watched, he speculated about the rocky surface, which from here looked so smooth and even.

The two fine lines below the hole, which ran nearly straight down, were undoubtedly ruts, worn away by generations of snakes taking the same path year after year. But after that, their descent was made at a slanting angle, and he wondered if there were similar grooves worn in the cliff, pathways by which a man might ascend. Not that he would want to be that man. Jamie shivered at the thought. For a moment he considered asking White Fang about it, but when he glanced over the old man's eyes were closed. He must have fallen asleep watching the snakes crawl down the cliff.

He awoke when Jamie stood up. The sun was almost overhead, and he knew he would be expected home for dinner.

"Good-bye, Mr. White Fang," he said shyly. "I've had a nice time watching the snakes with you."

The old man blinked, then held out his hand.

"Good-bye. My grandson say you want to be friend. We see. Tomorrow night you come to Cheyenne powwow at rocks. Very fine dancing. Like old days."

Chapter Six

"OF COURSE, YOU MAY GO TO THE POWWOW," AGREED
Aunt Nora. "We'll all go. We do every year."

Jamie had hurried home as fast as he could, but
even then he was late. Everyone but Dick, who carried his lunch to school, was at the table. He had
made his excuses by explaining the fascination of
watching the snakes crawl down the cliff and had
ended with White Fang's invitation.

"Did you know about this powwow, Charley?"
asked Uncle Bill. "You didn't say anything."

"I didn't know," admitted Charley, laughing. "My
grandfather said about a week ago that it would be
soon, but he hadn't set the date. He's not giving us
much notice."

"Maybe it has something to do with the rattlesnakes," suggested Jamie shrewdly. "Maybe he was

waiting for them to leave the cave."

"Could be," agreed Charley. "But it's more likely he's been thinking about it and just decided on the spur of the moment that tomorrow would be a good day. He doesn't have anything to do with getting ready for a powwow anymore. He forgets that there's work involved. It means hunting out the costumes and preparing food and spreading the news. Some of the people may have other plans for tomorrow, but that wouldn't occur to Grandfather."

"He can't expect everybody to drop what they're doing on such short notice," said Uncle Bill. "Maybe he won't get a full house."

"Everyone will cancel other plans," Charley told him positively. "They all understand about White Fang. He's old and has to be humored."

"What kind of food do you have, Charley?" asked Aunt Nora curiously. "I've always meant to ask you. Outsiders aren't invited to stay for that."

"It's always served so late," explained Charley apologetically. "Beef, mostly. I guess it used to be buffalo in the old days. We never eat much before dawn."

"You're not going to be worth a lot come Saturday morning," said Uncle Bill. "Lucky that Dick's home from school that day."

"Oh, I'll be fine," Charley assured him. "It's not the first time I've been up all night."

Jamie was so excited about the powwow he could hardly wait. Even though Charley gave him a lesson that afternoon on saddling a horse, he scarcely paid full attention. It was only when he was on Sal's back and galloping around the corral that he was able to put the powwow from his mind.

"When can I ride outside the fence?" he asked Uncle Bill later. "Sal is getting awfully tired of going around in circles."

"Someone will have to go with you the first few times," Uncle Bill told him. "Maybe tomorrow, if we're not too busy."

But when the next morning arrived, no one was free to take him on his first ride. Both Uncle Bill and Charley had chores to attend to. Dick was in school, and since they had run out of salt, Aunt Nora had to drive into Lame Deer to get some. She invited Jamie to go with her, but he refused. A long, bumpy jeep ride couldn't compete with one on the back of the white mare, and perhaps Charley or Uncle Bill might finish early.

After she drove away, he began to think he had made a mistake. The ranch house was deserted, and again there was nothing to do. He decided to walk down to the rocks and see how preparations were coming along for the powwow.

To his surprise, White Fang was not there this morning. Then he remembered that the festivities would continue until daybreak. It would be too much for the old man to spend both night and day at the rocks. Someone had probably convinced him that he must stay home and rest. Or perhaps Charley was wrong, and as a former medicine man there were preparations he must make.

Without White Fang's presence, the circle within the three rock walls seemed a little frightening. It was so very still, with not even a breath of wind. The sun had not yet climbed high enough to peep over the eastern rim, and after the warmth outside, the shadows felt cool and a little clammy. Jamie had never touched a snake, but he thought that their skins must feel the same way. He had an inclination to leave, then he told himself he was being silly. There was nothing here that could hurt him, unless it was a rattlesnake. Perhaps there were a few stragglers that were just now inching down the cliff.

He could feel his heart pounding as he stared at the wall. Today there was no movement on its surface, no tiny pencillike lines inching downward. No heavy greenish-yellow bodies dropped the last few feet to the ground, but somehow he could not overcome his uneasiness.

"You're a baby!" he said loudly, and his voice came whispering back in an echo from the rocks. "Baby!"

He thought of the boys he knew at school, the ones he had wanted to make his friends. They wouldn't have been afraid of an empty cave, even if it once had been inhabited by rattlesnakes. The snakes were gone. They had left yesterday, spreading themselves across the countryside in their summer search for food.

He made himself walk deliberately into the circle

and then toward the cliff with the round dark hole near the top.

"Here's where they slid to the ground," he muttered to himself. "Now let's see. They came sort of to one side, so maybe there's a rut."

He reached up with his hand, suppressing a shiver as he touched the rock. It was hard and unyielding, and his fingers did not linger long enough to feel for any groove that might have been there.

"It's too high to see," he told himself in a relieved tone. "I'd have to jump or find something to stand on. Maybe if I walk along a way I can see one of their trails."

He walked halfway down the side of the cliff, staring upward as he went. There was no movement anywhere. The snakes were gone, and his courage began to return. When he was directly below the place where the cave must be, he stopped. High above him, concealed by a slight bulge, was the rattlesnake den. It would have to be deep, for the book said the snakes must be protected from freezing. Perhaps it curved into the cliff, for that would give even more shelter.

He tried to imagine how it must look in winter when it was filled with coil after coil of greenish-yellow bodies. It must be crowded to capacity, for rattlesnakes lived as long as twenty-five years, and the females produced as many as twelve young each year. It would have to be a very big cave to hold so many, especially since the book said there was often a strip of ground that the snakes avoided. They left a clear area, several feet across, and no snake would cross the boundaries. It could be in any part of the cave, but it was always shunned by all. Beyond that area the snakes would appear again. To Jamie, this was every bit as remarkable as how they found their way back to the same den each fall, but the book had given no explanation.

He stared up, trying to read the answer, but suddenly he drew back in terror. There had been no movement, but he had seen something red and glowing just above his head. The eye of a snake, staring down at him? He stepped back a few feet and the red was gone. There was only the rough brown of the rock's surface.

After a moment, he went back to his original position, and he saw it again. It did not move. It lay motionless, and somehow he did not think it was alive. Something was caught in the rocks just above his head. Besides the scarlet dot, there was also a little white, unmistakable against the brown.

It must be some rock plant, he decided, grown from seeds scattered by a bird. There were bushes and clumps of grass growing on the other two cliffs. It was only this side that lacked vegetation. But bushes had green or tannish leaves, and leaves usually appeared before flowers. This thing, whatever it was, had only specks of red and white.

He reached warily up as far as he could, but it was still out of his grasp. For a moment he stood undecided. Then he found a fair sized rock lying loose on the ground, and by pushing and rolling, he managed to get it in position just below the cliff. It teetered unsteadily when he stood on it, but when he braced his left hand against the cliff, it held still.

He was afraid to touch the thing with his hand, so he found a stick, climbed onto the rock again and began poking about in the cliff above his head. At first nothing happened, then without warning something brown tumbled to the ground with a plop. For a moment Jamie stayed where he was, staring fearfully. When the object did not move, he jumped down and picked it up.

It was a small leather bag, much like the one White Fang carried. It was closed with a leather drawstring, and the side was ornamented with bead- and shellwork.

"A medicine bag," he whispered. "Somebody has lost his medicine bag."

But how could it have found its way ten feet up the side of the cliff? There was only one answer. Someone had carried it. The cliff wasn't inaccessible after all. There must be a way to the top. Probably the snakes had, as he suspected, worn grooves in the surface, and someone had used them to ascend. It had to be an Indian, of course, because no one else would carry a medicine bag. But why would he want to climb up to a rattlesnake den?

He carried the bag back to the place where he and White Fang had sat the first day he came here. By now the sun was peeping over the cliff, and the boulder that they had used as a backrest was no longer in shadows. Jamie was shivering a little, and the warmth felt good.

He sat on the ground and turned the bag over in his hands. It was very dusty, and he shook it to get rid of some of the dirt. It gave off a muffled clink and rattle. The beadwork was beautifully done, and when he looked at it carefully he saw that the design was that of a snake, coiled to strike. There were dark beads that he hadn't noticed before. The snake's body was made of them, and the eyes and extended tongue were red. The snake had white fangs, and there was another white object that Jamie thought looked rather like a shield.

He wondered to whom the bag belonged, and if, like a wallet, there might be a name inside. When he tugged on the strings, more dust rose to fill his nostrils, and he dumped the contents on the ground beside him.

They were disappointing. There were four crumbling rattles from a rattlesnake's tail, four small white stones, and a pile of dust that once might have been seeds or grasses. There was no name at all, nothing to identify the owner.

It was not until after Jamie had replaced the rattles and stones that he remembered what Charley had told him. White Fang's medicine bag was the only one left on the reservation today. Then who could be the owner of this one?

Chapter Seven

AFTER MUCH DELIBERATION, JAMIE DECIDED TO GIVE the medicine bag to Charley and ask him to find the owner. It would be better to do this when the two of them were alone. Like White Fang, the older Cheyennes might feel that a medicine bag was sacred, nothing to pass from hand to hand or talk about. Obviously, whoever dropped this relic while climbing the rocks had come by it illegally. Maybe he had even taken it from a coffin. Jamie didn't want to be mixed up in anything like that. The best thing to do was to turn the whole matter over to a member of the tribe.

It was harder to do than he imagined. When he got home Charley's old car was gone. Uncle Bill had sent him on an errand, and as soon as he got back the two disappeared to some distant part of the ranch.

Aunt Nora returned and prepared a meal, but there was no time to talk with Charley then. He and Uncle Bill were too concerned with a sick sheep. They hoped it was not something that would spread to the rest of the flock, and they both seemed so preoccupied that Jamie decided his discovery would have to wait. He took the medicine bag to his room and hid it in a drawer under his clean socks and shirts.

The school bus dropped Dick off at four o'clock, and after he had eaten four slices of bread and jam and drunk two glasses of milk, Aunt Nora asked if he would go riding with his cousin. Much to Jamie's surprise, he agreed. Dick hadn't paid much attention to him before.

"But we can't go far," he added. "I've got chores to do and it's Friday. Remember I get the car tonight, Mom. I've got a date."

"Tonight's the Indian powwow," Jamie reminded him. "Are you bringing your date to that?"

"Not a chance," said Dick positively. "You see one powwow, you've seen them all. I don't know how Charley puts up with it. Charley's cool. So are a lot of the others. They don't need that old stuff from the buffalo age. They really swing when they want to."

Dick was a good teacher. He loved horses, and he showed Jamie many things that he hadn't learned from riding around the corral by himself. Some of them, like not galloping uphill, Jamie had read earlier that afternoon in the book on horsemanship, but it was reassuring to hear them from an expert. It was fun to ride in the open and not be confined by a rail fence, and Jamie was disappointed when Dick said it was time to head home.

Preparations for the night's festivities were under way, for as they neared the Indian rocks he could see there were several cars parked nearby. Behind them on the road a horn tooted wildly, and Dick turned to make sure that Jamie pulled Old Sal over to the edge. A truck filled with Cheyenne rattled past, scattering gravel with its tires. Dick's horse shied a little, but Sal continued on undisturbed. Jamie leaned forward to pat her neck. Sal was a wonderful horse, the best. She wasn't afraid of anything.

It seemed to him that they would never get away from the house that evening. He had rubbed down both horses, Dick's as well as Sal, fed the baby animals, and set the table for Aunt Nora as fast as possible. But no one else appeared to realize this was a special night. The only thing that made it different was Charley's absence from the table. He hadn't waited to eat supper before joining his people at the rocks.

"You've worked up quite an appetite, Jamie," Aunt Nora told him approvingly. "But you don't have to eat so fast. There's plenty."

"I didn't want to keep you waiting," he explained. He was always hungry these days and ate everything that was served to him. He told himself that it was because Aunt Nora was such a good cook. "The powwow might get started before we're through."

"It will," said Uncle Bill dryly. "Any minute now we'll be hearing those drums, and they'll keep on all night, too."

"You won't miss a thing," Dick assured him, reaching for the potatoes. "All the dances look alike. You can't tell one from another. You can walk in and out any time."

"Dick's right," agreed Aunt Nora. "I suppose the Indians can tell a difference, but they look pretty much the same to us. We'll drive down in the truck after your uncle has watched the news on TV and I've cleaned up the kitchen. A half hour of it will be about all you'll want."

"Is that all they do? Just dance?" Jamie was surprised. "I thought powwow meant talk."

"I think it did once," agreed Uncle Bill. "And maybe, later in the evening after the visitors have gone, somebody may make a speech."

"White Fang probably," said Dick. "Telling the others what a big man he used to be."

"I'm sure he was a big man," said Aunt Nora reprovingly. "Now he's an old one, and I think the tribe deserves a lot of credit for honoring him the way they do."

"You can't tell me the young ones don't get a kick out of this, too," insisted Uncle Bill. "Some of those young sprouts put everything they've got into their dancing."

The drums started as they got up from the table.

Their deep voices carried clearly over the distance between the rocks and the ranch house, and they made a little thrill run down Jamie's back. These were real Indian drums, and the drummers were real Cheyenne, one of the fearless tribes who had roamed the plains a hundred years ago. The Cheyenne had been allies of the Sioux and had defeated the soldiers at the Little Big Horn. Tomorrow, maybe even tonight, he must start one of the books he had brought about Custer.

Occasionally the drums would stop, but in a few minutes they would begin again. *Dum—dum—dum.* And sometimes *dum—dum dum.* Jamie could hardly wait until Uncle Bill shut off the television and said that they might as well go.

By now there were so many cars around the rocks that they had to park the farm truck some distance away and walk in.

"Watch out for rattlers," said Aunt Nora nervously.

"Don't worry tonight. The noise will have driven them away," Uncle Bill reassured her.

The area within the rock walls was filled with the yellow glow of a central fire that flared high into the night sky. In addition, spotlights from two parked trucks added to the illumination. A dance was in progress when they arrived. The participants circled the fire, while the drummers, off in the shadows of the eastern wall, beat out the rhythm and chanted in unison.

"Over here," said Uncle Bill, and he led Aunt Nora and Jamie to a space below the southern cliff where a handful of white spectators had already gathered.

The Indians who were not taking part in this dance had massed themselves against the opposite cliff. Jamie grinned to himself in the darkness. If Aunt Nora and the others only knew that the rock behind them was the one used by the rattlesnakes when they went back and forth from their den, they wouldn't be so calm. He decided not to mention it but concentrated on the dancers.

Both men and women were dancing. There were children, too, and some of them, Jamie decided, were among the best dancers. At least they were the most vigorous. Although they all moved in a slow circle about the fire, every person performed his own steps, sometimes in a straight line, sometimes in small circles. Many wore anklets of feathers and bells that jangled clearly above the sound of the drums and the chanting voices.

Jamie had never seen such brilliant colors or elaborate costumes. There were feathers everywhere, in a rainbow of dazzling hues. There were red feathers and purple, green and blue and orange feathers. No bird could have ever grown them. They must have been dyed. Some were displayed in warbonnets, others in anklets, while some appeared in circles like spreading peacock tails on the rear of a dancer's costume. There were women in long brown or white dresses, heavily beaded and fringed, with beaded bands around their heads. Others wore everyday clothes, brightened by strands of beads or beaded headbands. Some of the faces were painted with black or red slashes or white circles, and Jamie remembered the expression "painted savages" from his reading. In the books they had sounded fierce and scary, but these faces were not frightening. Of course, they were not painted for war. This was a show, a festival, a theatrical affair, and everyone was having a good time.

The drums stopped abruptly, and the dancers walked out of the light and into the shadows.

"How do you like it?" asked Uncle Bill.

"Fine," said Jamie, and then began acknowledging introductions as Aunt Nora presented him to the white people standing nearby.

"Next is the Old Man's Dance," called a voice that seemed to echo through a tunnel. Someone near the drummer's section was using a megaphone.

By twos and threes, figures began emerging from the shadows to take their places by the fire. This time the costumes were not so flamboyant. Several of the men wore ordinary shirts, open at the throat, and Levi's. But there were strands of beads about their necks, and a few undyed feathers thrust into headbands. Others had buckskin shirts and moccasins. Last of all, White Fang came into the firelight.

White Fang wore a beaded shirt with a medallion hanging down his chest and leggings that came up to his thighs. His face was painted red, and a single black feather was thrust in his gray braided hair.

As soon as he had taken his place, the drums began. This time the beat was slow, and there were no elaborate jumps or skips by the dancers. The old men circled the fire four times, shuffling along sedately, their heads bending and rising stiffly as they went.

The crowd was respectfully silent, and when the drums stopped, the Cheyenne broke into enthusiastic applause.

"Well," said a familiar voice beside Jamie. "I see you got here. How do you like it?"

It was Charley White, who didn't look like himself at all, and Jamie had to look twice to make sure. Perhaps it was because he was concealed behind so much paint. There were zigzag streaks of white across his bare chest and back, black lines across each cheek and white circles around each eye. He wore beaded leggings, and a breechclout with two heavily beaded flaps that fell down in front and back. A scarlet cloth was tied around his head, with a tall black feather standing up behind.

"Do I look funny?" Charley's voice was amused. "I'm the real thing. Grandfather did the paint job himself."

"I think you look fine, Charley." Aunt Nora answered, for Jamie was too surprised to find his voice. "But won't you get cold without a shirt?"

"I'm tough," Charley assured her. "Besides, you work up a sweat when you dance."

"That doesn't look like an eagle's feather." Jamie stared at the glistening black feather thrust into the scarlet band.

"I'm not a Sioux," explained Charley. "Only the Sioux insisted on eagles. After the Cheyenne joined up with them, some of our warriors adopted eagle feathers, too, but before that we used crow feathers. Roman Nose, one of our most famous chiefs, had a warbonnet with forty crow feathers in the tail. He was quite a man."

"He must have been," agreed Jamie respectfully. He remembered reading that each feather in a war bonnet represented some deed of valor. "How about the others?" he asked. "The ones with bright colors. What tribe are they?"

"Everybody here is Cheyenne," said Charley, grinning. "They've just seen lots of movies and go to lots of intertribal powwows."

"Oh." Jamie felt a little disappointed. He would have liked to have seen the Cheyenne as they were originally. "Why doesn't your grandfather wear a warbonnet?" he asked. "Is it because he's a medicine man?"

"No," said Charley. "Lots of medicine men had warbonnets if they were warriors first. But you had to be a sharp character to be worthy of a warbonnet. You had to prove yourself before you put one on.

White Fang was born when the battles were about over. He doesn't think he's earned the right to wear one."

"But there's lots of them out there," insisted Jamie. "And the men are younger than your grandfather."

"Times change," said Charley, grinning. "Anybody can wear one now."

"The next dance is for the warriors of the Elk Society," called the voice through the megaphone. "All Elk warriors dance."

"That's me," said Charley. "The only time I remember I'm an Elk warrior is when we have a powwow."

The dance of the Elk warriors was similar to the first one Jamie had seen, except that it included no women. The participants ranged in age from White Fang to boys eleven or twelve. The older men moved slowly, but the young ones again danced with intricate steps and many turnings.

There was one thing, however, that distinguished this dance from the others. Every dancer carried two notched sticks, like the ones White Fang had shown him. When they were rubbed together, they gave off a dry rattling sound, audible above the drums, and not unlike the warning sound of a rattlesnake.

After this there was another mixed dance, followed by one for maidens only. Then the voice through the megaphone said that the members of the Crazy Dog Society would dance next.

"Seen enough?" asked Uncle Bill. "Are you ready to go?"

"I am," said Aunt Nora promptly. "I'm getting cold, even with my sweater. It's just more of the same, Jamie. It will go on all night."

"I guess so," he agreed reluctantly. Even if it was the same, he would have liked to stay longer.

It wasn't until he had turned down his covers and climbed into bed that he remembered the medicine bag. It must have belonged to one of the dancers he had seen that evening. He wondered which one.

Chapter Eight

JAMIE DIDN'T TRY TO READ THAT NIGHT. THROUGH the open window he could hear the drums going on and on, and he wished he were back there, watching. He turned off the light and tried to remember everything he had seen. The brilliantly dyed feathers had been beautiful, but his thoughts kept coming back to Charley with his beaded leggings and painted chest, to White Fang with his buckskin shirt and the single crow feather in his gray braids. That was the way the Cheyenne had really looked.

The next thing he knew, it was morning and the drums had stopped. He jumped out of bed immediately. Already he had learned that in this house there was no loitering. Aunt Nora didn't cook for stragglers. Anyone who arrived at the table late had to eat cold food out of the refrigerator.

At breakfast, Dick was so lavish with his praise about the way Jamie had conducted himself on yesterday's ride that Uncle Bill said he might venture out alone.

"But stay on the road," he added. "If you get lost, give Sal her head. She'll bring you home."

"Maybe I'll ride down to the rocks," said Jamie. He looked at Charley. "Did your grandfather come this morning, or did he sleep in?"

"He's still there," Charley reported. "He wouldn't go home at all. Maybe he thought some tourist would come by, and since he's all dressed up, it would be a good time to have his picture taken."

For a moment Jamie considered taking the medicine bag to White Fang, but he decided against it. There was no telling what the old man would do. He might even have a heart attack.

Sal carried him surely to the rocks, and when they arrived Jamie let the reins drag on the ground, the way Dick had shown him. The mare would stand when the reins were dropped, but Dick had warned him that not many of the ranch horses were trained this way. It was called ground tying, and Jamie thought it was just one more proof that Sal was an exceptional horse.

White Fang was there, just as Charley said he would be, but his eyes were closed. He was sitting on the ground, facing the ashes of last night's fire. He still wore the beaded shirt and medallion, but now the red paint, which had covered his face last night, had streaked and settled into the wrinkles. It gave him a curious, striped look.

Jamie sat down beside him, hoping he would wake up, but White Fang gave no signs of doing so. He continued to snore noisily through his half-opened mouth.

The circle within the rock walls looked very different today from the way it had last night. There were scattered scraps of paper on the ground and empty soft drink bottles dropped here and there. For lack of something else to do, Jamie decided to clean it up. It didn't seem right for the spot, which had been hallowed ground for some ancient people, to look that way.

He picked up the papers, wadding them into a big ball to be disposed of, and collected the bottles in one place. As he finished, he saw that White Fang's eyes were open and the old man was watching him suspiciously.

"Bottles belong Cheyenne," he accused. "Get money for bottles."

"Sure," Jamie agreed hastily. "I just put them all in one spot. When Charley picks you up tonight, he can put them in his car."

White Fang did not answer. For a long time he looked at the pile of empty bottles, and Jamie wondered if he was figuring up the amount of the refund.

"You like powwow?" he demanded suddenly.

"Oh, yes." Jamie came back and sat down on the ground beside the boulder. "I wish I could have stayed longer. Did you make a speech later on?"

White Fang nodded solemnly.

"After whites go, I make talk. Others talk. Good powwow."

"I thought you and Charley had the best costumes," confided Jamie eagerly. "Some of the others were pretty, but they weren't real, were they?"

White Fang shook his head scornfully.

"Where Cheyenne get purple feather? Green feather?"

"Did you dress like that every day?" asked Jamie. "Or just on special occasions?"

"Man has best clothes. Plain clothes," answered White Fang. "Plain clothes every day. No beads on moccasins. No beads on shirt. Put on best clothes for battle, for dances."

Jamie nodded. Whites followed similar customs.

"I thought the dance of the Elk warriors was the best," he said. "I liked the part where you all made the sticks sound like rattlesnakes. That must have been hard."

White Fang seemed pleased. To Jamie's surprise, he fumbled on the ground beside him for the carved sticks he had used in the dance.

"You mean I can touch them?" Even when they were held out to him, Jamie hesitated. He wouldn't want to do anything again to upset the old man.

"Touch," agreed White Fang. "Snake sticks not sacred. Every Elk warrior make own snake stick."

"Can they call the snakes with them?" Jamie ran

his finger up and down the length of carved wood. The grooves that made the noise were deep, and there were too many to count.

"Only holy man talk to snakes," said White Fang solemnly.

"But that's you," insisted Jamie. "You're the medicine man, the holy man. You must be able to call them."

"No," objected White Fang instantly. "Am holy man no more."

He jerked the sticks from Jamie's hand and dropped them on the ground. It was obvious that he wished to end the subject, but Jamie didn't want him to go back to sleep. The long morning stretched before him. He wanted White Fang to keep him company.

"I really liked your powwow," he said hurriedly. "I hope you have another one soon."

White Fang did not think the subject worthy of discussion. His eyelids began to flicker. Then, without warning, they were steady and the black eyes in the paint-filled wrinkles regarded Jamie suspiciously.

"Why you come here?" he demanded.

"I've been sick," said Jamie. "The doctor thought the fresh air would be good for me."

White Fang brushed away the explanation angrily. It was not what he meant.

"Why you come here?" he repeated. "Why you sit with White Fang? Make talk. White Fang old man. Today young have ears only for young. Not seek wisdom learned by old."

"I don't know anyone around here my age," admitted Jamie. Then, realizing that didn't sound too complimentary, he added, "But that wouldn't make any difference. I don't get along too well with kids, anyway."

"Why?" The old man stared at him suspiciously.

"I don't know. I guess they don't like the same things I do." When White Fang's eyes seemed to demand it, he went stumbling on. "You see, I'm not very good in sports or things like that. The other kids are. And half the time I don't know what they're talking about, and all the things I like to talk about, they aren't interested in."

"What things?" demanded White Fang.

"Oh, just stuff," said Jamie uncomfortably. At the moment he couldn't think of anything to say.

"You not like most boys," announced White Fang after a long pause. "My power grows weak. But I know. Maybe your calling comes early."

"My calling?" repeated Jamie stupidly.

"It was so with my brother, Round Stone." White Fang squinted straight ahead, as though trying to peer into the past. "Round Stone baby name. No harm to say out loud," he added quickly.

"What calling?" repeated Jamie, for the old man had fallen silent.

"Round Stone calling of holy man," said White Fang slowly. "Long before time for vision, he hunt sacred herbs. Dig *looski* bulbs. Gather special barks.

Sweet grass. Woman's work. Make other boys laugh to see."

"You mean your brother didn't have any friends?" asked Jamie in surprise. "The other kids just laughed at him?"

White Fang nodded soberly.

"That's the way it is with me," confided Jamie. Before he knew it, it was all coming out: the humiliation of being called "Genius," just because he had innocently carried around a few books; the deep hurt when he was always the last to be chosen on a team in gym; the exclusion from the parties and after-school activities of the other boys.

White Fang did not interrupt. He did not even glance in Jamie's direction while he was speaking, but at least his eyes remained open. When finally the account came to an end, the old man spoke, but not of the things Jamie had been talking about. It was of his brother, Round Stone, and it was as though he was continuing where he had left off before.

"Wherever tribe go, wherever women set down tepee poles, always same," he said. "Round Stone alone. Old men watch from lodge. Maybe they think that one get power early. Only think. Never say. Women busy. Not care. Boys shoot arrows at target every day. Take many arrows to make warrior. Round Stone stop. Want to shoot arrows. Boys laugh. 'Ha, ha. Round Stone carry sacred bulbs. Women's work. Go away.'"

"What kind of target did they use?" asked Jamie curiously.

"Set up log." Within the paint-filled wrinkles, White Fang's old eyes glittered with something like pleasure. Perhaps he was remembering when he himself was young and had practiced with a bow. "Put feather on top. Look like enemy. Each boy shoot four times. Four sacred number."

Then, without warning, his eyes closed and his head fell forward on his chest. As White Fang began to snore, Jamie shook his head ruefully. Last night had been hard on the old man. Probably he would sleep the rest of the day.

He got up and started for Old Sal. He might as well go back to the house.

Chapter Nine

THERE WAS NO CHANCE TO GET RID OF THE MEDICINE bag that day, for Uncle Bill sent Charley home shortly after noon. Since it was Saturday, Dick was there to help, and Uncle Bill said that a man who had danced all night couldn't be expected to work all day too. Charley protested a little, but not too much, and soon he drove away in his noisy car.

The medicine bag would keep, Jamie told himself. Then he forgot about it, for Dick invited him to ride along and help mend a fence that needed repair. Jamie was pleased. The ride yesterday had been at Aunt Nora's request, but today the idea was Dick's.

"How'd your helper turn out?" Uncle Bill asked Dick, when they finally sat down to supper. "Jamie catch on pretty fast to mending fence?"

"He did fine," agreed Dick promptly. "I'm going to teach him to milk a cow tomorrow."

"Oh, no, you don't," objected Aunt Nora quickly. "Milking the cow is your job, Dick Bennett. You're not going to try sloughing it off on Jamie."

"It wouldn't hurt him to learn," insisted Dick. "I took over the milking when I was his age. Everybody ought to know how to milk a cow."

"I'd like to," agreed Jamie quickly.

"So long as Dick doesn't forget that it's still his job," agreed Aunt Nora reluctantly. Then she looked around the table brightly. "Tomorrow I have something special planned for Jamie."

"What?" they asked in unison.

"When we drove in from Billings, Jamie wanted to see the Custer battlefield, but we didn't have time to stop," she told them. "I promised I'd take him, and I thought tomorrow might be a good time to do it. Wouldn't you two like to come along? We could take a picnic."

"Not me," declined Dick promptly. "I've got plans."

"I don't think I'll go," said Uncle Bill. "I've already seen it, and there's plenty to do around here."

"Jamie?" Aunt Nora was still smiling, but it was evident that she was a little disappointed.

"Oh, I'd like it, Aunt Nora," he assured her quickly. "There's nothing I'd rather do."

He went to his room early that night. If he was going to visit the Custer battlefield tomorrow, he had better read one of the books he had brought. It was interesting, but when he heard his aunt and uncle come upstairs, Jamie closed the book and turned off his light. Already he had discovered that if he read until midnight he couldn't make himself get up the next morning.

Usually he fell asleep immediately, but tonight was different. He kept remembering White Fang's brother, Round Stone, the boy who had no friends. What did he look like, Jamie wondered, and was he ever able to overcome his problem?

He must have dropped asleep very suddenly, for one moment he was lying there, staring into darkness, then it wasn't dark anymore. He was looking into a spot of sunlight, like a picture that might appear when he pushed the button on a TV set.

He saw a circle of brown tepees set in a rolling valley, with a small creek running through the middle. There were cooking fires in front of each dwelling, and Indian women in long, fringed dresses busied themselves with pots boiling over the flames. The sides of one of the tepees had been rolled up, and inside sat four old men. They wore buckskin shirts, beaded with porcupine quills, and medallions hung down their chests. From time to time they stirred the air or brushed away flies with fans made from crow feathers.

There were dogs everywhere, large ones and small. They were drawn by the odors from the cooking pots, but although they hovered hungrily, as close as they dared, none barked. Some small children, who were playing in the creek, were not so silent. They shouted and laughed as they splashed in the water.

Behind the camp, on a gentle rise that led to the grasslands beyond, a pony herd was grazing. Closer at hand, but well back from the lodges, three boys were practicing with bows and arrows. Their target, tied upright against a tree, was made of wood and bore some resemblance to the figure of a man. It had no arms or legs, but slight indentations in the upper part could have been a neck, and the bulbous swelling above looked a little like a head, especially since a feather had been thrust into the buckskin thongs that held it in place.

Each boy shot four arrows, one after another, before yielding his place. One, whom the others called Bear Sits Down, was especially adept. He placed all four of his arrows close to a smear of paint that marked the heart of the wooden man.

"You win again," admitted one of the others ruefully. "I think I'll quit shooting against you, Bear."

"I practice every day, Talking Crow," explained Bear. "You only shoot at the target when you feel like it."

"Bear Sits Down is training to take the place of Crazy Head, when our great warrior gets too old to go into battle for the Cheyenne," said the third boy, laughing.

"Why not replace Little Wolf?" suggested Talking

Crow slyly. "He is our first chief."

"Someone has to take their places someday," argued Bear Sits Down, undisturbed by their teasing. "Why not I? Black Legs here could be good if he'd only practice more. So could you, Talking Crow."

"I'd rather pull rabbits from their holes," admitted Talking Crow. "When you do that, you have something for the stewpot."

A fourth boy came walking up to them and stood shyly, waiting to be noticed. In his arms was a bunch of small purple flowers, still attached by their long stems to round brown bulbs.

"Well, if it isn't Round Stone," said Black Legs scornfully. "Been picking flowers again? Every time I see you, you've got some kind of flowers in your hands."

"This is *looski*." Round Stone reddened a little. "I found it blooming, so I dug it for my mother. I didn't take off the flowers because I wanted her to see that I dug the right bulb."

"They still look like purple flowers to me," insisted Talking Crow. "And why should you dig them? That's women's work."

"They're hard to find unless they're in bloom. And the flowers wilt so soon they might be gone by tomorrow. My mother makes *looski* bulbs into poultices for my father, White Buffalo. He uses them to heal wounds."

"White Buffalo is a good medicine man," said Bear Sits Down. "When my brother, Strong Wind

Blowing, got a Shoshone arrow in his back, White Buffalo healed the wound with one of his poultices."

"That would have been *looski,*" agreed Round Stone eagerly. He smiled at the three boys, but none of them smiled back.

"Then his woman should dig the roots," declared Black Legs, frowning. "That is proper. For a boy to walk around carrying purple flowers looks silly."

The three turned back to the target, and after a moment Round Stone continued on to the lodges.

The picture disappeared, and Jamie turned over in bed. He had been dreaming about the boy White Fang had told him about. He had wanted to know what Round Stone looked like, and he was disappointed. Of course, there was no truth in dreams. He was sure the figure he had dreamed about bore no resemblance to White Fang's brother.

How silly the boy had looked with his armful of purple flowers, the bulbs trailing down his brown legs. The others were right. It wasn't a very manly way to act, and his excuse about helping his mother had sounded pretty feeble. If it was a woman's place to gather bulbs and herbs, maybe Round Stone should have left it to her.

Jamie yawned and went back to sleep.

The next morning Aunt Nora drove him to the Custer battlefield. It was not at all what Jamie had imagined from reading his book. He had envisioned a small space, with the Little Big Horn River running through the middle. Instead it covered a large

area and was composed of one hillock after another.

High on one of the rises was a building, sparkling white in the morning sun, that contained a museum. Nearby was a fenced area, enclosing a tall monument, where the remains of the dead soldiers eventually had been buried in a common grave. Behind that was a more modern cemetery with markers lined up in military precision, but Jamie was not interested in that.

Instead he was fascinated by the white painted stakes that were scattered throughout the slopes and that barely peeked through the grass. They carried no names, but each marked the spot where it was believed some cavalryman had fallen in battle. Some were clustered in small groups, but many were alone and far apart. There were also scattered gray logs standing upright in the ground to a height of two or three feet, and the folder Jamie had bought at the museum said they represented spots where Indian sharpshooters had taken up their positions.

Jamie was glad he had read the book last night. Otherwise he wouldn't have known the reason for the battle.

A hundred years ago, in the 1870s, the government had decided to confine the roving bands of western Indians on reservations. This, of course, was to leave their lands free for settlement by whites.

The Sioux, composed of several different tribes, had united under Sitting Bull to resist. They were joined by their friends, the Northern Cheyenne. It made an unwieldy party, many thousands in number, but they stayed together because alone they were too weak to accomplish anything.

No one knew why Custer divided his forces, but he sent several companies, under Major Reno, to attack the lower end of the Indian encampment while he himself concentrated on the upper end. Reno's forces had advanced upon the camp of the Hunkpapa Sioux, but he had been forced to retreat. His men were held under fire for two days on the hillocks above the river.

Custer himself, with two hundred twenty-five men, rode down to attack the opposite end, occupied by the Cheyenne. In the face of the enraged tribesmen, it was a rash thing to do. Within the space of a few hours, not one of his command remained alive.

Those were the barest facts, but standing on the rise above the museum, the whole thing seemed to come alive to Jamie. Here on this spot brave men had died, white men and red, and each had thought his way was right.

Aunt Nora good-naturedly let him follow the numbers on a map that marked the circumference of the battlefield, but she didn't go herself. She said it was a long walk, and she'd rather wait in the car and read.

Jamie left the trail and wandered down the rough slope to the south. Here was where the Cheyenne had been attacked, where they and their friends the Sioux had won their most famous victory. White Fang's elder brothers had fought here, and one of them had given his life.

His boots made a hard crunching sound on the dry ground, and stickers from weeds flew up and clung to his pants legs. One or twice he encountered a white stake, almost hidden in the grass. Custer's men had scattered, each trying desperately to save himself.

The sun was hot on his head and shoulders, but there was a little breeze. It stirred the grasses and brushed against his warm cheek. It made a little lonely sound that left Jamie curiously uncomfortable, and he decided it was time to go back to the car.

Aunt Nora looked up from her book when he arrived.

"Seen enough?" she asked. "I thought we might go down to the river to eat our lunch."

Jamie agreed that was a good idea. He wanted to get out of here. The uncomfortable sensation that had come over him on the hillside refused to leave. It was almost as though the wind had been trying to tell him something.

Chapter Ten

APPARENTLY UNCLE BILL HAD SPENT SUNDAY MAP-ping out the week's work. He and Charley discussed it over breakfast the next morning, then the two of them left together in the jeep.

"I forgot to tell you, Jamie," Charley shouted over his shoulder before they drove off. "There's a surprise waiting for you at the rocks. You'd better ride down there right away."

Jamie nodded and started for the corral. He wondered what kind of surprise could be waiting.

As soon as Old Sal rounded the cliff and came to a halt, he didn't have to wonder anymore. A boy about his own age, who had been sitting on the ground beside White Fang, jumped to his feet and came hurrying to greet him.

For a moment the familiar feeling of uncertainty

flooded over Jamie. Would this stranger like him? Would he be friendly? Then the feeling vanished, for the boy was grinning.

"Hi," he called. "Grandfather wanted me to come with him today, and Charley said he'd send you down."

The boy was an Indian. He wore Levi's and a faded plaid shirt. His black hair was cut short like Charley's.

"Hi," said Jamie. He slid from the saddle and let the reins drag on the ground.

"I'm Horse," announced the boy. "Charley's brother. I saw you the other night at the powwow. Charley says you come here every day to talk to Grandfather."

"He doesn't talk much," said Jamie ruefully. "But what he says is interesting."

"He's a great old guy." Horse nodded, and his dark eyes regarded Jamie with approval. It was evident that he was prepared to like anyone who approved of White Fang. "But you're right. He doesn't talk unless he wants to."

"Your name is Horse?" asked Jamie. "Just plain Horse?"

"It's Horace really," admitted the boy, making a face. "But Horse is better. Sometimes I tell the goofy tourists my name is Running Horse or Red Horse or something like that. It makes them feel good. If I make up a fancy enough name, they give me two bits extra to pose for a picture."

"Pose for a picture?"

"Sure." Horse laughed heartily. "Goofy tourists are always trying to take pictures of Indians when they get close to a reservation. I guess they think we're freaks or something. So we make them pay."

"I wouldn't pose for somebody who thought I was a freak," said Jamie.

"Oh, we get a good laugh over it," Horse told him carelessly. "They're the freaks, you know, not us. You should see some of them. And listening to them is even funnier."

They walked over to where White Fang was sitting.

"Hello, Mr. White Fang," said Jamie. "I'm glad you brought your grandson with you today."

White Fang looked up, but he didn't bother to reply.

"Well, what shall we do?" demanded Horse. "I guess we could go have a look at the picture cave."

Jamie agreed. He thought it might be a good idea if Horse saw how the drawings of his ancestors had been desecrated. Maybe he would tell the Cheyenne and they could do something about it.

However, Horse was not surprised to see the chalk marks and the scratches over the faded red drawings.

"Goofy tourists," he said scornfully. "You see what I mean?"

"Don't you care?" asked Jamie in surprise.

"What good would it do? So long as Grandfather

doesn't find out, it doesn't matter. You haven't told him, have you?"

"Oh, no," Jamie assured him quickly. "I was going to tell Uncle Bill about it, but I forgot. Maybe he could stop people from coming here."

"Grandfather would like that," said Horse. "I think he just stays here to keep an eye on things. He really doesn't care about having his picture taken. He says this is a holy place and that somebody is buried here. Somebody important."

"Who? Where? In this cave?" Jamie stared at the rocky walls, then at the hard stone floor beneath his feet.

"Probably nobody is at all," admitted Horse. "It's just an idea of Grandfather's. Our people used to believe that when somebody got very old, he was able to sense a place where somebody had been buried. He didn't have to know about it beforehand. It just sort of came to him. Of course we know that isn't true, but Grandfather still hangs on to the things his people believed. We don't argue with him."

"But there's no place around here to bury anyone," objected Jamie. He looked down at the granite-strewn earth below. "You couldn't get a shovel in there anywhere."

"They didn't do it that way. In the old days, the Cheyenne used to bury dead people in caves."

"But there's only two caves here. This one and the one where the rattlesnakes hibernate."

"Oh, they always blocked up the entrance with

rocks," said Horse. "They didn't want anybody to disturb the body. I guess they were pretty good at it, too. After they'd filled in the entrance, nobody could tell it had been there."

"Do you think there's someone buried in this cave?" Jamie looked around at the rough walls surrounding them.

"Not a chance," Horse told him quickly. "Not with the pictures. That made this cave holy. And the one with the rattlers is too high up. But there could have been other caves in the cliff that were filled up. It's a likely spot. That's probably what Grandfather's thinking about when he says someone is buried here."

Jamie agreed. He walked over to the nearest wall and began running one finger across the letters that said, "Gary loves Sheila."

"Look," he cried in excitement. "The chalk rubs off. And it doesn't hurt the picture underneath. Why don't we clean up the cave?"

"It wouldn't be too much fun," said Horse reluctantly. "But I guess we could. There's nothing else to do."

There was little they could do about the deep scratches, but they began working on the chalk immediately. Jamie used his big handkerchief, and Horse took off his shirt and used that.

As they rubbed, they talked. Horse was full of questions about Disneyland and Hollywood. He wanted to know about movie stars he had seen in

pictures and took it for granted that because Jamie lived in California he met them daily on the street.

Jamie, in turn, was disappointed in the answers to his own questions. Horse didn't own a bow and arrow, and he'd never used one. Jamie didn't tell him about his dream, but he did ask whether Horse had heard the names Bear Sits Down, Talking Crow, or Black Legs. Horse never had, but he said they were fine names, and the next time he met a goofy tourist he would say that his own name was Horse Sits Down. He thought it had a nice sound.

He had, of course, heard about Round Stone.

"He was Grandfather's brother. He got killed at the Little Big Horn. Grandfather never knew him, because Round Stone died before he was born. But you'd never know it to hear him talk. You'd think that they were pals."

"Was Round Stone a medicine man too?"

"He was going to be when he grew up, but he got killed too soon. I guess maybe he was about our age when he died." Horse stopped rubbing at chalk marks and looked at Jamie speculatively. "Grandfather must really like you if he told you about Round Stone."

"He didn't tell me very much," said Jamie honestly. "Just that he liked to gather herbs and bulbs to make medicine."

"Did he tell you about the time Round Stone went on a buffalo hunt and got caught by the Fox warriors?"

Jamie shook his head, and Horse launched immediately into the story.

"Well, Round Stone and some of his friends went on a buffalo hunt with the tribe. The Fox warriors were in charge that day and—" he broke off, frowning a little. "You wouldn't know about that, though, would you? You see, the Cheyenne had three warrior societies, the Fox, the Crazy Dog, and the Elk."

"That's what you are," said Jamie eagerly. "An Elk. At least your grandfather and Charley are. I saw them dance at the powwow."

"That's right." Horse nodded. "On each buffalo hunt one of the warrior societies was in charge. They led, and everybody else had to follow. If anybody sneaked ahead of them and got caught, it went pretty hard on him. They killed his pony and his dog and tore his clothes to pieces and whipped him and broke his bow. They were pretty tough in those days."

Jamie agreed that they must have been.

"But kids were always trying to outsmart the lead warriors on a hunt," continued Horse, and his eyes sparkled in appreciation. "So one day, Round Stone and some of his friends tried it. The others got away, but Round Stone was caught."

"What did they do to him?"

"Nothing," said Horse, grinning. "But they scared him plenty. And he probably got laughed at by the others, and that made it worse. The Fox warriors who caught him said he was just a kid and not worth bothering about. They sent him home to his father.

I never could find out what his father did about it. Grandfather would never say."

"He was lucky," admitted Jamie thoughtfully. Somehow, the story as Horse told it, did not coincide with the image he had already formed of Round Stone.

At last the walls were cleaned, and they looked quite presentable. The ancient red drawings were much clearer without the dust and chalk marks.

"Too bad we can't tell Grandfather how hard we worked on his holy place," said Horse, as they started down the trail. "But I don't want him to know what the goofy tourists had done."

"Do you come here often with your grandfather?" Jamie asked eagerly. He couldn't remember a morning he had enjoyed so much.

"No. Only when there's no work to do at home, and that's not often."

White Fang watched them approach, and the black eyes in their folds of wrinkles were approving.

"Good boys," he said. "Clean holy place. Make pictures of old ones bright again."

"How did he know?" demanded Jamie, staring at Horse in amazement.

Horse shrugged, then he began to grin.

"I guess he saw the dirt on my shirt. And your face is pretty dirty. Grandfather doesn't miss much."

Jamie suddenly realized the sun was directly overhead. They had spent all morning in the cave. Now it was noon and Aunt Nora would be expecting him home to eat. He was hungry, but he didn't want to leave his new friend. Horse had accepted him in a way no one had ever done before.

"I have to go home for dinner," he said reluctantly. Then, without even thinking of the consequences, he added, "Why don't you come with me? Charley's there."

"OK." Horse accepted immediately. "Your horse will carry double. Did they give her to you to ride while you're here?"

"Yes." For the first time Jamie looked at Old Sal, seeing her as she must appear to the Cheyenne boy. She was old and careful, a horse reserved for novices. "I don't know much about riding. They gave her to me because she's supposed to be safe."

"You're lucky," said Horse cheerfully. "I don't have a horse."

All the way up the road, his new friend kept chattering away. Jamie answered yes and no, but inside he was worrying. What had he done? He had never invited someone to lunch before in his life. Even if there had been anyone to invite at home, it would have meant securing permission from his mother first. And she would want to know all about the proposed guest, his habits and who his parents were. Stuff like that. Today it had seemed the natural thing to do, and he had done it. Now he wondered what Aunt Nora and Uncle Bill would say. Would they be angry and perhaps drive away the only friend he had made?

They turned Sal loose in the corral, but Jamie didn't take off the saddle. She might have to go right out again, returning Horse to the rocks.

"I've never been inside your house," said Horse, staring around curiously. "Once I rode over with Charley when he forgot something, but I waited in the car."

Through the screen, they could see that the family was already eating. Aunt Nora, Uncle Bill, and Charley were seated at the big table in the center of the kitchen. Jamie opened the door and took a deep breath.

"I made a new friend," he said bravely. "His name is Horse. I asked him to come home for dinner."

"Hello, Horse," said Uncle Bill. "Come on in and shut the screen. The flies are bad today."

"We wondered what was keeping you," said Aunt Nora. "Goodness, you both look like you've been rolling in the dust. Take your friend to the bathroom to wash up, Jamie, while I put on another plate."

"And use soap," ordered Charley. "Plenty of it. You look like a couple of pigs. How'd you get that way, anyhow?"

"That's what we want to talk to you about, Uncle Bill," said Jamie. All the heaviness had gone out of him, and he was smiling so widely it almost hurt his face. "Just wait till you hear why we had to get so dirty."

Chapter Eleven

THAT NIGHT JAMIE DREAMED ABOUT THE INDIAN BOYS again. The picture came as it had before. The darkness was gone and he was staring into the light.

He saw a vast prairie that went on and on to where the horizon made a straight line against the sky. There were many horses—ponies really, for they were too small to be called horses. Astride each one was an Indian, and it was a normal day, not a special occasion, for they wore no ornaments or decorated trappings. All of them were men, young men in the prime of life, but riding at the fringe of the group were several boys.

Bear Sits Down was one of them. He rode a shaggy pony, small but sturdy. Talking Crow and Black Legs rode similar mounts. They used no saddles, and their bridles were of rawhide, made in the form of a headstall with a bit for the animal's mouth. Each carried bow and arrows.

"I wish it weren't the turn of the Fox warriors to lead the hunt," complained Talking Crow. "They're so slow. The buffalo will be gone before we get there."

"They're no slower than the Crazy Dog or Elk warriors," insisted Black Leg. "And they're cautious. Wrapped Braids heads the Fox warriors today, and he's never led a hunt that returned without meat."

"There will be no meat today if he doesn't hurry and find a herd," said Talking Crow. "I think we ought to ride off on our own and have a look around."

"You know that's not allowed," Black Legs reminded him, but he smiled and his voice was mocking. "No one must ride ahead of the warriors who head the day's hunt."

"We nearly got caught the last time we tried it," said Bear Sits Down. "And you know what the punishment is."

"The penalty for going ahead of the scouts is to have your horse or dog killed or to be pony whipped or have your clothes slashed to pieces and your gun or bow broken," answered Talking Crow in a singsong voice. He seemed to think it was amusing. "It's a rule made by old men."

"Careful," warned Black Legs, as a fourth pony trotted up beside them. "Go away, Round Stone," he ordered. "We're not picking flowers. We're hunting buffalo. Ride with someone else."

"What we're thinking about doing is too scary for you," taunted Talking Crow. "Go back to your mother and help her pound bulbs."

"I'm not afraid," insisted Round Stone doggedly. "I'm not afraid to do anything you do. And I know what you're planning, too. You're going to ride ahead and not wait for the Fox scouts to return and tell us where the buffalo are."

"What makes you think we'd do a thing like that?" asked Bear Sits Down. "It's not allowed."

"You've done it before," said Round Stone. "You think nobody knows about it, but I do. You were lucky not to get caught."

"How do you know?" Talking Crow pulled his pony close to Round Stone's, his black eyes narrowed in anger. "Who told you?"

Round Stone stood his ground. He did not waver beneath the angry glare.

"I just know," he insisted. "If you're going again, I want to go with you."

"Wouldn't you be afraid?" asked Bear Sits Down. "You'd be breaking a law, and you know what will happen if you get caught."

"I know," said Round Stone.

"Come on, then," agreed Bear Sits Down indifferently. He began planning their strategy. "When we come even with that clump of bushes, ride into them. When all the men have passed by, we'll circle around. There are swells in the ground to give us cover, and eventually we can get ahead. If we're lucky, they won't notice."

The four boys let their ponies lag behind the larger party. When they were even with the bushes, they guided their mounts into the cover. It was not a thick stand, and any of the riders who happened to look back would have seen them, but no one looked back.

They waited there for some minutes, then rode out. Instead of following the others east, they made an angle north. Bear Sits Down, Talking Crow and Black Legs laughed among themselves at the great trick they were playing on the marshals of the day's hunt, the Fox warriors, and they rode hard and fast.

Round Stone rode a little behind. He kept all expression from his face, but a small muscle throbbed at his temple. There was determination in the set of his jaw, as though he might be out to prove something to the others.

Eventually the leaders halted. They were holding a consultation as Round Stone rode up.

"Are you sure we did right in going this way, Bear?" demanded Talking Crow.

"Nobody can be sure of that. But at least we're ahead of the others now. Look at the ponies. They're winded from running. Besides, there could be buffalo here, just as well as anywhere else."

"The ponies are spent," said Round Stone in a worried tone. "Mine needs to rest. I don't want him to die under me."

The others ignored him.

"I say we scout around on foot a little," suggested Talking Crow. "See if there are any signs of a herd and where they might have gone."

The three slid to the ground, and Round Stone did the same. The ponies stood with hanging heads. Their matted coats were dripping wet.

"We'll each take a different direction to scout," said Bear Sits Down. "Look for wallows and chips. Then come back here where we've left the ponies."

Without comment the others walked away, spreading out like the half-opened ribs of a fan. Talking Crow continued due north. Bear took a course a little to the east, with Black Legs next to him. It left only due south for Round Stone. It was the direction taken by the large hunt party, but he started out, his eyes scanning the ground carefully. There was the same determination on his face as before, but now that he was alone, his eyes showed a little apprehension.

For a long time he continued on. No one had said how far each should go before turning back. From time to time Round Stone stopped to look over his shoulder. The others were not in sight. Even the place where they had left the ponies was concealed by the waving prairie grasses.

From a distance the ground looked flat and level, but at close hand it was actually composed of gentle swells. At the top, one could see a short distance. In the hollow of the undulation, only the sloping sides were visible.

Round Stone halted at the summit of one of the swells. For a moment the fear that was within him showed plainly on his face. Riding toward him were two men. They saw him at the same instant and both kicked their horses ahead.

Round Stone stayed where he was, and after that first moment all emotion was erased from his face. He stood stoically waiting.

The hooves of the approaching ponies stirred up little saffron puffs of dust. The long black hair of the riders blew backward from their shoulders, and the sun glistened on brown skin, damp with sweat. They came to a halt as they reached the boy and sat frowning down at him.

"What have we here, Mosquito?" The taller of the two riders addressed the other. "He's a Cheyenne. I've seen him around the camp."

"A puppy. A Cheyenne puppy," agreed Mosquito contemptuously. "He is son to White Buffalo and brother to Walks at Night."

"Does White Buffalo, the holy man of the Elk warriors, and Walks at Night, one of their promising young braves, know that their young puppy has tried to scout the buffalo herd ahead of the day's leaders?" asked the tall man. "Perhaps they are the ones to be punished for breaking the law."

"No, Wrapped Braids," Round Stone spoke up bravely. "My father and brother do not know. I am the one to be punished. Here is my bow. Break it. Shall I take off my clothes so you can tear them to pieces? Or will you beat me with your whips?"

"Where is your pony?" Wrapped Braids ignored his questions. "And your friends? You did not come here by yourself. When puppies try to outsmart the scouts, they always run in packs."

"I am alone," Round Stone insisted, looking at the ground. "I have no friends."

"He will be easy to track," said Mosquito, nodding in the direction from which Round Stone had come.

"Follow us," ordered Wrapped Braids sternly. "Do not think you can escape."

The two riders kicked their ponies ahead, and Round Stone turned and began retracing his steps. He walked slowly, and now that he was alone fear had returned to his face. As he walked, he examined his bow, letting his fingers run down the length of curved wood lovingly, as though he might be caressing it for the last time. But when he arrived at the place where he had left his pony, his face was blank and the bow was again slung across his shoulder.

"Your friends are gone," said Mosquito. "Their tracks are here, but they did not wait for you. Do you want to tell us their names?"

"I have no friends," insisted Round Stone, and there was a ring of sincerity in his voice.

"It is in your favor that you do not name others." Wrapped Braid's eyes showed approval. "We have decided that you are too young for punishment by warriors. Wait with the women until the hunt is over. Then tell your father and brother of how you broke the law. They will know how to deal with you."

The picture was gone as suddenly as it had appeared. One moment Jamie had been looking at Round Stone and the two Cheyenne warriors. The next he was staring into darkness.

He knew why he had dreamed this dream. Ever since Horse had told him about Round Stone's experience on the buffalo hunt, he had felt that something was wrong. It couldn't have happened the way Horse said.

In the first place, Round Stone had no real friends. The others wouldn't have invited him to take part in their fun. He must have tagged along. And he would have done that only in an effort to gain their respect.

Jamie knew all about trying to gain someone's respect. Often at school he had tried to take part in games that were beyond his physical strength. Every time he had made such a poor showing that he wished he had never tried in the first place.

Poor Round Stone. Jamie knew exactly how he felt.

Chapter Twelve

THE DAYS BEGAN TO GO BY VERY RAPIDLY. DICK graduated from high school, and they all attended the ceremony. After that he was home every day, helping with the work.

Jamie found that his own jobs were increasing, too. He had learned to milk the cow, although Aunt Nora saw to it that Dick did not turn the chore over to him every day. Once he and Sal even helped move a herd of cattle to a different field. He mailed the last of his schoolwork to the principal and finished the books on Custer.

It grew increasingly hard to write a daily letter to his mother, and they compromised on twice a week. Often she called on the telephone just to hear his voice. She was worried that he might have an accident on his horse or get sick, and Jamie had to assure her again and again that Sal was perfectly safe and that he had never felt so well in his life. He was careful to keep his remarks guarded and not bring up anything to cause her alarm.

Horse had managed only one more trip to the ranch. Charley said their father was keeping him very busy at home. But every day Jamie rode to the rocks. Often he and White Fang just sat together in companionable silence, but sometimes they had conversations. The old man told him of the herbal cures practiced by his people; how *looski* root poultices healed gunshot and arrow wounds, and how snow blindness was cured by puffing snowflakes in the eyes, at the same time repeating special words.

One day Jamie asked him how the Cheyenne had happened to unite with the Sioux in their battle against the whites. White Fang had taken his time about answering, and when he finally spoke his old voice quavered with anger.

"Cheyenne and Sioux always friends. Cheyenne not want to fight. Sioux not want to fight. Want to be left alone. Some try white man's way. Go to soldier forts. Not hunt buffalo. Eat spotted cow. Pah! Belly always hungry. Wear white man's blanket. No good. No good. Blanket cold. Fall to pieces. Cheyenne leave."

"Then what happened?" From his reading Jamie already knew, but he wanted to hear White Fang's story.

"Cheyenne make camp on Powder River. Forty

lodges," reported the old man angrily. "Cold. Snow deep. Not expect soldiers. But they come. Steal Cheyenne horses. Set fire to tepees. Kill. Men, women, babies. Kill all. Few get away. Hide in mountains. When sun closes great eye, Cheyenne warriors steal back horses. People travel four suns. Not many robes. Little food. Seek encampment of Oglala Sioux. Crazy Horse big chief of Oglalas. Take Cheyenne in. Give food. Blankets. Weapons. Make welcome. Old chiefs make talk. We go to join Sitting Bull and Hunkpapa Sioux. Together we fight our enemy."

Jamie nodded soberly. It was the same story he had read in the books. He had thought then that the Indians had just cause for their anger. After listening to White Fang, he was even more convinced.

That night he came across the medicine bag in his bureau drawer. He had almost forgotten about it. It must be very old, he decided, turning it over in his hands. The beadwork was finer than any he had seen in the museum at Custer's battlefield. The red eyes and the protruding red tongue of the rattlesnake looked very real. He was sure it was valuable. Tomorrow he must remember to give it to Charley. In the beginning, he had been waiting until the two were alone, but lately there had been too much to think about.

There had been no dreams about the Cheyenne boys for several weeks, but tonight they came again. Jamie was very tired, and his head had scarcely touched the pillow when the dreams began.

He was looking at winter. No cooking fires burned in the circle made by the brown tepees, and all traces of old fires had been covered by the snow that fell steadily from the dark sky. The camp was huddled against a cliff to give some small protection from an icy wind that blew out of the north. It was night, and the entrance flaps were tightly closed.

Then, without warning, a gunshot came from the blackness outside the camp. It was followed by others. Men shouted, and there were the sounds of horses neighing a protest to the prick of steel spurs, the scrape of sabers sliding from scabbards, then more gunfire.

A tepee burst into flames, and by its light the startled Cheyenne began pouring out of their dwellings. Three sides of their camp were surrounded by mounted cavalrymen, yelling, shooting, swinging sabers. The first to emerge fell instantly, victims of rifles or swinging steel, but the Indians came so swiftly from the lodges that the soldiers had no time to reload or swing their swords again. Some escaped, running into the open, squeezing between horses or ducking below their bellies, to disappear into the night. Meanwhile the snow about the camp was stained red with the blood of Cheyenne men, women, and children, and the night was hideous with their cries.

Jamie awoke with a shudder. The whole thing had been so vivid, his ears still rang with shouts and screams and the sounds of gunfire. It had been a terrifying experience, and he was glad it was only a dream.

He remembered reading that if you wanted to make sure a dream wouldn't continue, the thing to do was turn over. He rolled to the other side, but it didn't work. In a few moments he was dreaming again, but this time the dream was different.

He was looking into a crowded lodge. Some of the people must have been recently arrived, for there was the usual commotion of greeting guests, women running here and there, offering comforts, the newly arrived protesting that they did not want to cause trouble.

There were only women and children in this dwelling, and many of the smaller ones were crying.

"It is the snow," explained one of the mothers of a sobbing child. "We had no pony, and his feet feel frozen. Small wonder, for he had to walk the last mile himself. I could not carry him and his smaller brother, too."

"Soon the medicine men will be finished with the men, then they will come here," said one of the women who obviously lived there. "The Sioux have many good medicine men. They will take care of our friends, the Cheyenne."

"We had a medicine man with us—White Buffalo," said the Cheyenne mother wearily. "But perhaps he was killed by the white soldiers. So many of our people were. In the long walk to find the winter camp of the Oglalas, others died also. I do not know how many of us are left."

"My father, White Buffalo, still lives." Round Stone stepped out of the crowd of shivering children to reassure her. "I am sure he will come to this lodge as soon as he can."

"There, you see." The Sioux woman tried to speak cheerfully. "In the meantime, the stew is hot. Our friends, the Cheyenne, will feel better with hot meat in their stomachs."

She ladled out steaming portions from the pot boiling over the central fire, and other women began passing it to their guests. Some of the children stopped crying as they were offered food.

Round Stone went back beside the wall of buffalo hide where the boys had gathered. He did not try to join them but stopped at the edge of the group, eating silently.

"I cannot eat," complained Bear Sits Down. "I cannot see the spoon in my hand. My eyes are blinded by the snow."

"When he comes, the medicine man will take care of that," Talking Crow assured him. "And of my feet too. I did not know they were frozen until I came into the warmth. Now it is as though sheets of fire were running up my legs."

Round Stone moved a little closer.

"I know what my father does for snow blindness and for frozen feet." His voice was timid. "I do not know the proper words to say, but the treatment is always the same. If the pain is very great, and you want me to try—"

"I do not mind pain," said Talking Crow sharply. "I am almost a man."

"I would be glad to have you try." Bear Sits Down accepted eagerly. "The pain is nothing, but it is hard not to see."

"Don't let him, Bear," warned Talking Crow. "Round Stone is not a medicine man. What does he know? He may cause even more damage. He could make it worse."

"What harm can he do?" argued Bear Sits Down logically. "He said himself he did not know the words, only the treatment. Try it, Round Stone."

Round Stone put down his half-filled horn spoon and went outside the lodge. When he returned, he carried his fur cap loaded with fresh snow. He squatted down in front of Bear Sits Down and, filling his mouth with snow, puffed it gently into the red staring eyes. Time after time he repeated the process. Once he had to go outside for more snow.

Talking Crow kept insisting that Round Stone was causing even greater harm to the blinded eyes. But when Bear Sits Down cried, "I see light. It must be the fire," he was silent.

At last Bear joyfully announced that the cure was complete. His eyes still stung, and the whites were bloodshot, but he was no longer blind.

"Let him treat your feet," he urged Talking Crow.

"I'll wait for White Buffalo," Talking Crow said stubbornly.

"Have it your way," said Bear Sits Down, picking up his cold stew. "I'm glad I didn't." He smiled at Round Stone.

"Where is Black Legs?" Round Stone asked. He seemed pleased that Bear Sits Down had let him minister to his snow blindness.

"He's dead," said Bear Sits Down, and the smile faded from his face. "The pony soldiers killed him."

Once again Jamie awoke. This time he got up and went to the bathroom for a glass of water.

He was not afraid, as he had been in the dream about the battle. It was rather like welcoming old friends to dream about Round Stone and Bear Sits Down and Talking Crow again. It was too bad about Black Legs, but it was a wonder any of them had come through that fearful attack by the soldiers.

He wondered why, after so many weeks, he had dreamed of the Cheyenne boys again, and decided that there was a logical explanation. Somewhere he had read that dreams were a composite of a person's thoughts, and White Fang had been telling him about these events in the lives of his people only today.

Chapter Thirteen

On the fourth of july the cheyenne held a rodeo on their reservation, and Uncle Bill said they would all attend.

"It's going to be awfully dusty," Aunt Nora reminded him. "And hot, too. Are you sure you want to go?"

Jamie held his breath. He had never seen a rodeo, much less one that was staged by Indians.

"It would be just as hot at home," Uncle Bill insisted. "And I think Jamie would like it."

"Maybe he'll want to enter one of the races," said Dick. "He's getting so good on Old Sal, I think he should be promoted to a better horse."

"Oh, no," objected Jamie quickly. "I like Sal, and she likes me."

He hoped Horse would be at the rodeo. He hadn't

seen his friend for almost a month. Charley said that their mother and the younger children were away picking berries. Every summer they left the reservation and journeyed to distant orchards and farms where they were paid for gathering crops.

When he asked Charley whether his brother would be back, Charley didn't know.

"He could be," he said. "It depends on where they are and how the fruit is holding out. But they'll be back pretty soon. Our father will need Horse to help with the hay."

The rodeo was held in a dusty field, surrounded by a ramshackle fence. Tiers of seats had been erected on one side to form a grandstand, and after paying their admission, the white visitors found places there. There were some Indians in the grandstand, too, the elderly who could not stand on their feet for several hours at a time. Able-bodied members of the tribe preferred to hang over the surrounding railings.

Across the field were other areas, more substantially fenced, that contained the wild horses, Brahma steers, and calves soon to be roped and tied in special events. That side of the fence was crowded also, but not by spectators. The Cheyenne, who sat on the top rails or pushed in below, were the contenders for the day's events. Jamie was surprised to see that their number included girls and young women as well as men and boys.

"There's White Fang," announced Aunt Nora after they sat down. "He's getting to look awfully old, Bill. It wasn't so noticeable the night of the powwow, under all that paint."

"Uh-huh," agreed Uncle Bill absently. He clapped his knee with his hand, and the crack made Jamie jump. "That one didn't even wait to get out of the chute. Look at him go!"

They had missed the opening, and the wild horse ride was already under way. These were animals that had not been broken to the saddle, and they made their objections to having a man on their backs known immediately.

Jamie held his breath as the horse, stiff legged, jolted up and down. For a second the sound of hooves striking against ground reverberated across the field, while the rider clung desperately with one hand, the other waving wildly. Then he went flying through the air to land in the dust, and the horse, with an indignant shake of his head, galloped off.

"No time on that ride," said Uncle Bill.

The rider picked himself up, recovered his hat, struck it against his side to remove the dust, and went limping back to the fence. He was received with much laughter and good-natured comments.

The doors of the chute opened to admit another horse and rider to the field, but Jamie didn't notice. He had leaned over Uncle Bill to speak to his aunt.

"Aunt Nora, could I go over and talk to White Fang a minute? I want to know if Horse got back."

"Let him go. Let him go," said Uncle Bill, impatiently pushing Jamie out of his line of vision.

"All right," agreed Aunt Nora. "But come right back."

Jamie squeezed past knees until he came to the end of the row, then made his way up the stairs to the section where the older Cheyenne were sitting. It was lucky, he told himself, that White Fang had an aisle seat. He had to wait until the ride was over, but when White Fang finally looked up he was in a good humor.

"Hello, Mr. White Fang," said Jamie. "Could you tell me if your grandson, Horse, is here today?"

"Horse here." The old head nodded proudly. "Horse in Cheyenne rodeo. Pretty soon he rope calf."

Uncle Bill and Aunt Nora were mildly pleased to hear that Horse was entered in a rodeo event, but Jamie was beside himself with excitement. He hoped his friend would win, and it was all he could do to sit through the rest of the bucking events and the squaw race that followed. Luckily the boys' calf roping was next on the program.

The boys were all under thirteen years of age. They rode out onto the field one at a time, and a calf was turned loose. They had to lasso the animal, jump from the horse's back, and tie the calf's legs securely while the judges recorded their time. It was hard to do, and because of their weight only a few of the boys were successful in throwing the calf at all.

Jamie was sure that Horse was the best of the entrants, even though his time fell short of some of the others. The flourish with which he spun his rope, the skill with which he downed the bawling calf and trussed up its legs were worthy of special recognition. He looked very jaunty today, too, in a red shirt with a beaded band around his head.

As soon as the results were announced, Jamie began begging to be allowed to join his friend.

"Well, I don't know." Aunt Nora hesitated, frowning. "They're all Indians over there. You'd be by yourself."

"What's that got to do with it?" demanded Uncle Bill impatiently. He pulled a dollar from his pocket. "Here, buy Horse a hot dog. Tell him we think he did fine."

Jamie had to go out the gate and circle the outside of the fenced area to reach the other side. He had passed the concession stands and was nearly there before the significance of Aunt Nora's words penetrated his brain. Today he would truly be an outsider. The only one he knew was Horse, and perhaps Horse wouldn't be glad to see him.

He paused, wondering if he should return to the grandstand. Two Indian boys, who had been buying popcorn, passed him as he stood there. They looked at him curiously, and he knew they were wondering what he was doing.

"I'm looking for Horse White," he called impulsively. "He's a friend of mine."

One of the boys shrugged indifferently, but the

other spoke over his shoulder.

"He's probably over by the chute. He was in the last event."

"I know," said Jamie proudly. "I want to tell him I'm sorry he didn't win."

Anybody could understand that, he told himself. He had explained his presence, and perhaps the two boys would spread the word to anyone who was critical.

As he neared the section of fence containing the chute, a group of boys started toward him. They had been contenders in the calf-roping contest, and one wore a red shirt with a beaded band around his head. Jamie stopped short. He should have thought of this. Today Horse was with his old friends. Maybe he wouldn't have time for a new one.

Then Horse recognized him and waved.

"Hi, Jim. You see the calf roping?" he called.

"Yes." Jamie's heart thumped so loudly he could hear it. "I just came to tell you it was cool. I thought you should have won."

The boys had reached him by this time, and they all stopped. He could feel their eyes resting on him curiously, but he kept looking at Horse's brown face beneath the beaded headband.

"I wasn't good enough," said Horse, laughing. "This is the winner, Pete Longtree. And this is Sam and George and Steve and Shorty. This is my friend, Jim Steele. He's spending the summer with his relatives."

At the change in his name, Jamie gave a start of surprise. Maybe Horse had decided that Jamie was a little like his own name, Horace, and that the shortened version was better. But he couldn't take the time to think about that now. The other boys were waiting, and he made himself look into their faces. Without exception, they were smiling good-naturedly.

"I sure wish I could ride like you and rope a calf," he told them wistfully. "But I'll never be able to."

"It just takes practice," said Pete Longtree.

"Jim lives in California," Horse said. "He's been to Disneyland lots of times, and he's seen some real movie stars."

"Not very many," protested Jamie. "And I don't know any. I just happened to see a few."

The boys looked at him respectfully.

"We're going to get a Coke," explained Horse. "Want to come?"

"Sure." Jamie's fingers closed over the bill in his pocket. "I've got a dollar. Uncle Bill told me to buy you a hot dog and to tell you he thought you did fine."

"Good," approved Horse. "We've only got thirty cents. We're hoping to find some goofy tourists."

Jamie fell into step beside him, wondering what he meant.

"We're too early," said the boy named Sam. "The goofy tourists are still in the grandstand."

"Awful hot up there," Pete reminded him. "The

sun really beats down today. Some of them will give up pretty soon."

"The rest of you should have worn something tied around your heads," complained Horse. "You don't look too authentic to me."

"Hey, there's a couple now," cried Steve in excitement. "Just coming out the gate. You talk, Horse. You do it best."

The boys began running, and Jamie hurried to keep up with them. They intercepted the man and woman before they had reached the area of parked cars.

"How," said Horse solemnly, pushing ahead of the group and extending his hand to the man. "You like um rodeo?"

For a moment the two looked startled. Then the man took Horse's outthrust hand and shook it. They were of middle age, and the woman wore very tight shorts and a bright blue blouse. Her too golden hair was elaborately dressed, with many curls and a high pompadour that extended well above the crown. The man wore a flowered Hawaiian shirt and carried a camera slung over one shoulder.

"How," he replied to Horse, a little self-consciously. "Yes, we liked the rodeo very much. Are you in it?"

"Me rope calf," admitted Horse, and Jamie had to bite his lip to keep from laughing. The white couple stared from one to another of the boys as though hypnotized. Probably, he told himself, they

had never spoken to real Indians before.

"Oh, Robert," cried the woman. "Aren't they darling? Do you suppose they'll let us take their picture? We don't have any close-up shots."

Horse drew back in pretended alarm, and the others began speaking with each other in a tongue that Jamie could not understand.

"Old ones say magic box take part of soul," protested Horse, covering his face with his hands.

"Nonsense," said the man briskly. "You don't believe that. It's not true, and you know it."

"No hurt?" Horse peeped out from between his fingers.

"Of course not, honey," said the woman. "I've just got to have their pictures, Robert. I had no idea the Cheyenne were so backward. People will never believe it when I tell them."

"OK," said the man a little wearily. He reached in his pocket and pulled out a handful of change. "Let's see. There's sixty-two cents here. If you'll stand still and let me take your picture, you can have it."

Horse spoke to the others in the strange tongue, and after a moment they seemed to agree and began lining up.

"Not you," said the woman to Jamie, who was on the outer end. "You stand away. We don't want a picture of a white boy."

"Him not white," objected Horse. "Him throwback to ancient captive, taken long ago by Cheyenne warrior."

"Really?" The woman looked at Jamie in awe.

"I don't believe it," declared the man. "But he's on the end, so we can always cut him off."

After the picture was snapped and the sixty-two cents had changed hands, the woman had one more request.

"Now tell me your names. I want to write them down on the back of the picture after it's developed."

"Me Horse Sits Down," said Horse solemnly. "Him Lame Deer. Him Little Wolf. Him Crazy Head. Him Two Moons. Him Roman Nose. And him"—he looked at Jamie, and his eyes sparkled—"him Lame White Man."

The woman wrote down the names with many delighted squeals. Then she and her husband continued on to the parking lot.

"Goofy tourists," said Pete in a disgusted tone. "You put on a good show for them, Horse. It was worth sixty-two cents."

"Why did you call me Lame White Man?" asked Jamie, as they started toward the concession stand.

"It was all I could think of," Horse told him, laughing. "Lame White Man was a real chief. Grandfather says he was very brave and fought with our people and the Sioux against Custer. I always try to give the goofy tourists real names. It seems like they get more for their money that way."

Jamie contributed Uncle Bill's dollar, which, combined with what they had, made enough for Cokes and popcorn for everyone. The ice had run out so the Coke was tepid, but Jamie thought it was the most delicious he'd ever tasted. The boys had accepted him as Horse's friend, and they took it for granted that he would return with them to the Cheyenne side of the fence.

Later, when they had a moment alone, he told Horse about the medicine bag he had found.

"I've been meaning to give it to Charley," he concluded. "But I wanted to do it when we were alone, and I keep forgetting. Whoever it belongs to must be awfully worried about it. If you could just ask around and tell him it's safe, I know he'd feel better."

"I don't know who to ask," admitted Horse. "So far as I know, Grandfather's is the only medicine bag in the tribe. They don't make them anymore."

"I think it's pretty old," said Jamie. "I opened it up, looking for a name, and the stuff inside has mostly turned to powder."

"Maybe it's Crow and not Cheyenne," said Horse. "A few of them showed up at the powwow late in the evening."

"I found it before the powwow. It was in the morning, and your grandfather wasn't there. He'd stayed home to get ready. We were both there the day before. That was the morning we watched the snakes leave their den and crawl down the rocks."

"Beats me," admitted Horse. "I'll nose around and see what I can find out. Except I don't dare ask Grandfather. He'd go up in the air if he thought some family had held out a medicine bag. They're supposed to be buried with the owner. That's why they're so scarce nowadays."

That evening, when Jamie wrote his letter home, he addressed it to both parents, not just to "Mother" as he had always done before. He was still too excited about the Indian rodeo to write about anything else, and he didn't think his mother would be very interested. But Dad would. He might even like it as much as he did a football game.

He hesitated a moment when he came to the end. Then he signed it, "Your loving son, Jim."

Chapter Fourteen

"Did your brother, round stone, get to be a real medicine man before he was killed?" asked Jamie.

To his delight, he had found White Fang in one of his rare talkative moods when he went to the rocks that morning.

The old man finished the last of Aunt Nora's freshly baked cookies that Jamie had brought along and wiped his mouth with his sleeve.

"Round Stone have vision," he said, peering inside the paper sack to make sure he hadn't missed anything. "Get secret helper. New name. No time to be holy man. Die too soon."

"What was his new name?"

"Not good to say name of dead." White Fang frowned fiercely. "Bring bad luck."

"But everybody says Crazy Horse's name and Sitting Bull's and Little Wolf's," protested Jamie. "I've even heard you say them. And they're dead."

"Sometimes man have two names," White Fang told him cunningly. "One name secret. Never say after dead. Other name not matter."

"Oh," said Jamie. He wondered if White Fang was telling the truth, or if had just made up the explanation on the spur of the moment.

"I tell you this," White Fang said grudgingly. "Round Stone's new name some like my name. Some different."

"Did it have something to do with snakes?"

"Maybe so," said White Fang reluctantly. Then after a moment, "Maybe not."

"How did he get it? Who gave it to him?" Jamie was determined to take advantage of White Fang's willingness to talk. There were lots of things about the Cheyenne that he wanted to know.

"Our father give new name. Round Stone go alone to seek vision. Very young. No other boy so young. Paint body special way. Spend four suns in buffalo-hide hut. Dark. No food. No water. Helper come to him. Make self known. After that, get new name."

"I bet the other boys were jealous that he beat them to it."

White Fang nodded solemnly.

"I bet after that they wanted to have him in their games." Jamie gloated a little over Round Stone's triumph. "If he got his vision earlier than anybody else, they'd know he was special. They'd all want to be his friend after that."

"No," said White Fang sadly. "Round Stone still alone. No friend. Not till day he die. Then friends Sioux. Not Cheyenne." Suddenly his face twisted into a grimace, and his bony hand grasped Jamie's arm. "You get Charley," he gasped. "Tell him come. Now."

"Are you sick, Mr. White Fang?" cried Jamie in alarm. "Can I do something? Maybe you'd better lie down."

The old Indian shook his head.

"Get Charley," he repeated, and after a moment Jamie raced to the spot where Sal was standing in the shade of the rocks.

Luckily Charley was working near the barn that morning. He did not stop to ask questions. When Jamie rode up and shouted, "Your grandfather wants you. I think he's sick," Charley dropped what he was doing and ran to his car.

"How bad is he?" asked Uncle Bill. "Think I ought to call the doctor?"

"I don't know," admitted Jamie. "He wouldn't tell me anything. Just that he wanted Charley."

"I'd better drive down to the rocks and see," said Uncle Bill.

As he watched the jeep follow Charley's old car down the road, Jamie wished that he had been invited to go along. After all, White Fang was his special friend. But he hadn't been invited, and there was nothing to do but wait for Uncle Bill.

Even when he returned, there was no news.

"Charley said not to call the doctor," he reported. "Old White Fang wouldn't hear of it. He said that he just wanted to be taken home to die."

"To die?" repeated Aunt Nora. "Die of what? Was it a heart attack?"

"Charley doesn't think so," said Uncle Bill. "The reservation doctor looked the old man over not long ago. He said White Fang had a heart like a horse. But, of course, at his age anything can happen. I told Charley to take him home and stay there as long as he was needed."

"White Fang was beginning to show his age," said Aunt Nora. "I told you that the day of the rodeo. Remember?"

"He was feeling fine this morning," said Jamie unhappily. "He talked more than he usually does. And he liked your cookies, Aunt Nora. He ate most of them. I only got one."

"There's certainly nothing in my cookies to bring on an attack of something," said Aunt Nora indignantly, as Uncle Bill and Dick began to laugh. "And if you two think so, you can just keep your hands out of the cookie jar."

Charley only stayed at home for a few hours. Early in the afternoon he returned to the ranch.

"I don't know what set him off," he told them. "Even though Grandfather didn't want him, we called the doctor. He couldn't find anything wrong. Grandfather's in fine shape, considering his age."

"What does your grandfather say?" asked Dick curiously.

"I'm afraid his mind's wandering." Charley looked a little embarrassed. "He says he has to die because a member of the family is angry. Of course, there's nothing to it. Nobody's angry about anything. He's just imagining things."

Jamie was very upset. He kept wondering if White Fang's sickness had something to do with their conversation that morning. True, the old man had seemed willing to talk, but Jamie had kept pushing him for more and more details, things that White Fang considered secret. Maybe he had gone too far.

He tossed and turned for a long time after he went to bed, and it was not surprising that he had another dream about the Cheyenne.

When it began, everything was very dark. It was not the darkness that comes from a starless night, but the enveloping blackness of a closet without windows. There was the feel of a shut-in closet, too, for the space was very small.

Gradually, Jamie's eyes grew accustomed to the change, and he could see Round Stone sitting with his back against a wall of skins, his bare feet touching the opposite side of the enclosure. He could not stand upright, for the bent willow wands, which made the structure, were not long enough. Many buffalo hides had been piled over them to keep out light and air.

Round Stone sat motionless, with closed eyes. He

might have been asleep, except that his cracked lips moved in prayer.

"Great Medicine," he whispered. "Make me a brave man and a good one. Four days and nights I have fasted alone in this place. No food or water have touched my lips. The only human voice I have heard has been that of your servant and my father, White Buffalo, when he comes by each evening to see that all is well. You have sent me a sign, but it was a strange one. No one else of our people has had the rattlesnake circle his medicine lodge, shaking its rattles. I do not know what it means, Great Medicine. I only know that you have seen me here."

His voice broke off suddenly, and he sat up straighter. Muffled by the thick hides, there were approaching voices.

In a few moments someone tore aside the buffalo skin that formed the door covering of the hut. As light poured inside, Round Stone shielded his eyes.

"My son," said White Buffalo. "The allotted time is at an end. For four days and four nights you have made medicine. Now you may come out."

Blinking, the boy crawled from the hut and staggered to his feet. He wore no clothing, and his whole body was painted with red clay. There was a black circle around his face and others around his wrists and ankles. A black sun decorated his chest and on his left shoulder appeared a black moon.

White Buffalo came forward and took him by the hand.

"Hoh, all Cheyenne," he cried, turning to address the small group that had followed him to the hut. "This is my son. He has withstood the trials and tortures of the four-day vigil. He has been seen by the Great Medicine, who has sent a sign. On the second night of his lonely vigil, a rattlesnake circled his medicine lodge, shaking its rattles. It was an omen and a promise. No rattlesnake shall ever harm my son. The rattlesnake has become his appointed helper and will stand guard over him. From this day forward, my son gives up his childhood name of Round Stone. He will be known as Fears No White Fanged Snake."

On the edge of the spectators, Talking Crow spoke to Bear Sits Down. Although his voice was low, it was scornful.

"What kind of a helper is a snake? When I make my medicine, I want a buffalo or at least a wolf."

"Hush," said Bear Sits Down, frowning. "He will hear you. Besides, Round Stone—I mean Fears No White Fanged Snake—is not so bad. He cured my snow blindness, didn't he?"

"It would probably have cured itself," insisted Talking Crow. "I think he's strange. He's stopped picking flowers, but who else would make a four-day vigil at the same time Sitting Bull holds a sun dance? It's disrespectful. Now that the Cheyenne are traveling with the Sioux, we should honor their leader. All the Sioux and Cheyenne are watching Sitting Bull's sun dance. There's practically no one here to see Round Stone come out of his medicine lodge."

"We're here," pointed out Bear Sits Down.

"Only because we were curious. We didn't think he would make it. Everyone else on the hillside is of Round Stone's own family."

White Buffalo had been praying to the Great Medicine, thanking him for noticing Fears No White Fanged Snake and for sending him a sign of approval. Now he turned back to the boy.

"This is your medicine bag," he said. "When I came to the outside of your hut the second night, and you told me you had heard the dry rattles of the snake through the buckskin hides, your mother began to bead the design. I have placed within it certain objects that will help keep you safe from harm. It is strong medicine. Keep it with you always."

Before the picture faded and Jamie awoke, he had a good look at the medicine bag that exchanged hands. The beaded design was of a snake with red eyes and protruding tongue. The snake had white fangs, and beside it was another beaded object in white that resembled a shield. It was identical to the medicine bag Jamie had found in the rock wall below the cave.

Chapter Fifteen

WHITE FANG WAS NO BETTER THE FOLLOWING DAY or the next. Charley told them he lay on his bed with his face to the wall, and when he spoke it was only to insist that he was going to die. He drank water willingly, but it took their combined efforts to coax him to eat anything.

"Maybe it was my fault," confessed Jamie one morning. He had followed Charley to the shed where he was making some repairs on the tractor.

"What do you mean?" Charley looked at him in surprise.

"Well, we were talking that day about his brother. The one who died in the battle of the Little Big Horn. And I kept teasing him to tell me things that he didn't want to."

"Don't worry about that." Charley turned back

to his work. "Grandfather tells just what he wants to tell and no more. And as for Round Stone, he likes to talk about him."

"But I wanted to know his real name. Things like that," said Jamie miserably.

"I used to ask him that myself." Charley ran his fingers up and down the threads of some kind of screw. "He'd never tell me. Only that it was a little like his own. Nobody knows Round Stone's real name. It was buried with him."

"Where was he buried?" asked Jamie curiously. He was relieved that his questions had not been the cause of White Fang's illness.

"Nobody knows that either. In a cave someplace. After the battle, his mother and father carried his body away for secret burial. Grandfather says that when the tribes moved on to get away from the army reinforcements that were on the way to rescue Reno, they weren't there. They caught up with the others later."

"It's funny how your grandfather knows all these things when he wasn't there himself," said Jamie thoughtfully.

"You don't know our people." Charley laughed. "Maybe we didn't write things down in books, but we're real historians. The word of mouth kind. Particularly when it comes to heroes. Round Stone was a hero, you know. He was about twelve or thirteen when he was killed. He'd ridden over to the Hunkpapa camp with some kind of message when they shouted the alarm that the soldiers were coming. The Hunkpapas weren't ready for them. So while the warriors ran for their horses, some Sioux kids rode back and forth in front of the camp to stir up a dust screen. Round Stone was there on his pony, so he rode with them. He was the only one killed."

"Then he was a hero," said Jamie.

He remembered what White Fang had told him. Round Stone had no friends until the day he died, and those friends were Sioux, not Cheyenne. Charley's story had a familiar ring, and he thought there might have been a reference to it in one of the Custer books.

That night he looked it up, and the account of the Sioux boys and their valiant ride to delay the action of the soldiers was there, all right. It was sketchily told, in only a few lines, and there was no mention of a Cheyenne having taken part. Perhaps the historians didn't know, or more probably they didn't think it was important.

Jamie thought it was important. He hoped he would dream about it, and he did.

He saw Fears No White Fanged Snake sitting astride his shaggy pony, which was not much larger than a big dog. His black hair flowed smoothly over the shoulders of his fringed shirt, but his legs were bare. Around his neck, suspended from a leather thong, hung the medicine bag with the beaded snake emblem. His father, White Buffalo, was standing beside the pony, giving instructions and Fears No

White Fanged Snake was trying, without too much success, to conceal his impatience.

"That is the message," said White Buffalo. "Carry it to Medicine Calf Pipe, the chief medicine man of the Hunkpapa Sioux. Are you sure you know their camp?"

"Yes, Father." Fears No White Fanged Snake nodded. "The Hunkpapas' is the last of the seven circles gathered together on the Greasy Grass."

"That is right," agreed White Buffalo. "It is only fitting that the Hunkpapa be the last, just as the Cheyenne camp is the first. They are the hosts, we are the guests. To reach it you must pass directly through the circles of the Arrows All Gone and the Miniconjou Sioux. Behind you, and back from the river, are our friends the Oglalas and the Blackfoot Sioux, as well as the Burned Thighs. You need not pass through their circles to reach the Hunkpapa. You can skirt the edges."

"Yes, Father." The boy's voice was dutiful, but a little weary, as though all these details were unnecessary.

"Our combined encampment is large." White Buffalo did not seem to notice. "There has never been such a large gathering before, as many as the stars in the sky. But it is necessary that the tribes of the Sioux Nation unite against the white man who comes to defile our sacred hills and kill the buffalo and take our land for their own. We, of the Northern Cheyenne, can do no less than join the Sioux against our common enemy. Soon, I think, the Southern Cheyenne may follow us. Their chief, Lame White Man, with his family, is already here."

"Yes, Father, I know." This time there was an open note of impatience in the voice of Fears No White Fanged Snake. White Buffalo heard it and broke off guiltily.

"I am growing old," he admitted. "I wander in my thoughts. Go swiftly to the Hunkpapa Sioux. Find the lodge of Medicine Calf Pipe. Tell him that last night, when I called to the wolf on the ridge, the wolf answered me. It was a sign, and soon there will be fresh meat on the ground. Sitting Bull, in his vision, saw white men falling into our camp like grasshoppers. Since Sitting Bull plans to move the tribes tomorrow, the white men will attack today. The wolf is never wrong. That is the message."

"Yes, Father," said Fears No White Fanged Snake again, and this time White Buffalo let him ride away.

The encampment was indeed extensive. Seven great circles of tepees, all facing east to greet the sunrise, extended along the river's bank. They were similar in appearance, but those of the Sioux were slightly taller and not so wide of base as the lodges of the Cheyenne. All had emblems—a sun, a moon, or jagged lines of lightning painted on the tough buffalo-hide covers.

Fears No White Fanged Snake guided his pony through the first circle, skillfully avoiding playing children and smoldering cooking fires. The sun beat down from a cloudless sky, and thousands of flies swarmed everywhere. He jerked at his legs to keep the flies from settling on his skin, but the pony seemed impervious to their bites. Perhaps they could not penetrate the coat, like thick, matted wool.

The air was filled with sweetness from some kind of grass that the women had stacked at the entrances of the tepees. From time to time the stacks were tossed about so the grass on the bottom was exposed to the sun's rays. Fears No White Fanged Snake seemed especially interested in the grass piles. Once he slowed his pony to look more carefully. Then, as though remembering his mission, he hurried on.

In every circle the scene was much the same; children playing, women going about their day's work, old men sitting in whatever shade they could find, talking together as they brushed away flies, young men sharpening arrow points or whetting the edges of stone battle clubs. A few were cleaning guns or extracting stuck cartridges, but there were not many guns. Bows and arrows were more plentiful.

The encampment extended several miles, and because it followed the curving course of the stream, the Cheyenne circle at the beginning was soon lost from view. In the benchlands above grazed a large pony herd, but it was impossible to see the line of mountains to the south because of a heat haze that shimmered dizzily in the air.

As he approached the last circle, Fears No White Fanged Snake raised his hand and called to a group of children playing in the dust.

"I seek the lodge of Medicine Calf Pipe."

Most of them only stared, but one boy pointed straight ahead. The lodge of the medicine man was at the opposite side of the circle. Fears No White Fanged Snake rode on.

The Hunkpapa camp was larger than the others. It took some time to guide the pony through the maze of cooking fires, children, dogs, and busy women. A group of old men chiefs, wearing porcupine trimmed shirts and eagle feathers in their gray braids, sat in the shade of an open tepee, gossiping. The sides were rolled up for ventilation.

When he reached the last tepee in the circle, Fears No White Fanged Snake dismounted. Several boys close to his own age were sitting on the ground. Like their elders, they were sharpening arrowheads, honing the points with stone.

"Hoh," said the Cheyenne boy shyly. "I am Fears No White Fanged Snake. I seek Medicine Calf Pipe. I bring a message from my father, White Buffalo, medicine man of the Cheyenne."

The boys looked up at him, smiling.

"He is not here," began one. "He—"

He was interrupted by a loud voice shouting an alarm.

"Hi-ya! Hi-ya! Every warrior to his horse. The pony soldiers come!"

"That's Gall," cried one of the Sioux boys. "Gall, our war chief!"

They jumped to their feet, dropping their arrows and turning to stare over their shoulders. Rapidly approaching from the river crossing was a cloud of dust. One or two horses could not have made so long a banner. It would take a large company.

The camp was in instant confusion. Children screamed, dogs barked, mothers called anxiously. Warriors had stopped readying their weapons and were now running for the pony herd. Old men shouted advice to which no one listened.

The next moment, a stern-faced Sioux, wearing a fringed vest, open to show his scarred chest, came running toward the boys.

"Young as you are, you must help your people," he told them swiftly. "There are a few ponies tethered here in camp. Mount them and ride back and forth before the beginning of the lodges. Stir up dust to make a screen so the soldiers cannot see. It may hold them back a little and give our warriors time to mount and arm themselves."

Eagerly, the boys ran to do his bidding. Their faces showed pride at being called on by the war chief.

"I'll ride, too," offered Fears No White Fanged Snake quickly. "I am a Cheyenne. Your enemy is ours."

Gall nodded approvingly before hurrying away to make ready for battle.

The boys lost no time. Only a few favorite ponies had been tethered inside the camp, but they each found one and came riding back. They carried no arms, for their mission was not to fight, only to delay

As they circled the lodge, the dust cloud made by the advancing soldiers was coming closer. It was not possible to see the blue coats of the riders in front. The boys wasted no time in looking but began riding back and forth, back and forth before the lodges, and as they rode they shouted the ancient war cries of their people.

"Hi-yi-yi," screamed the Sioux boys.

"Ah-ya, ah-ya," shouted Fears No White Fanged Snake.

There was an answering shout from the advancing soldiers, but only one. After that they continued on in silence, save for the pounding hooves of their iron-shod horses, which grew louder by the minute.

The ground was dry, and the feet of the ponies churned it into dust that rose in a great saffron screen to shield the camp. Back and forth, back and forth rode the Indian boys, so the dust had no time to settle but was carried up again before it fell to earth. It wrapped the riders in its gritty folds so they could not see, and sometimes the ponies stumbled against each other. But they were light-footed and regained their balance without falling.

The dust screen did not stop their ears, and from one side they could hear the sounds of the Hunk-papa Sioux preparing for war, from the other the pounding hooves of cavalry horses, now close enough so they were like drumbeats.

"Halt!" It was a man's voice and it spoke in English. "Dismount!"

The hoofbeats stopped, but the boys rode on and the dust screen continued to fill the air.

"Prepare to fire!"

Back and forth, back and forth rode the unarmed boys, five Sioux and one Cheyenne. If they understood what was happening, it made no difference. They rode to help their people against an enemy who sought to drive them from their land, to force them into a strange mold that was alien to everything they believed.

"Fire!"

The rifles cracked and spurts of hot iron pierced the saffron dust. The boys had to fall back. Unarmed as they were, they had no place in battle. Nor was there need. By now the angry Sioux were mounted and armed. They were riding out to meet the invaders in ever-increasing numbers.

The boys rode their lathered ponies into the circle made by the lodges, coughing and blinking to clear their noses and eyes. Their faces were proud and very happy, and they told themselves that they were lucky to be there. They counted themselves to be sure. Only one was missing, the Cheyenne boy. What had he called himself? Fears No White Fanged Snake.

"He was brave," said one of them. "Too bad he wasn't a Hunkpapa Sioux. I'd like to have known him better."

Jamie awoke, and there were tears running down his cheeks.

Poor White Fanged Snake! He had given his life without knowing he had gained a friend. Five friends, really. Five Sioux boys who would never forget the Cheyenne that had ridden with them in that dust cloud.

He wished that Bear Sits Down and Talking Crow could have been there to see how bravely Fears No White Fanged Snake had conducted himself. Of course, they would hear about it, but that wasn't the same thing. He would have liked them to know how the Sioux had accepted the Cheyenne as one of them. It was almost too much to ask, but maybe they had.

He turned over in bed and dreamed again.

This time it seemed to be the following day, for it was very early in the morning. He was looking at the Cheyenne camp. All was confusion. Women were taking down the lodges, sliding off the heavy coverings of buffalo hide, and rolling them into bundles; attaching the stout poles onto the carrying saddles of horses, so that when the animals walked the poles would drag behind. Cooking pots, blankets, clothing, and lighter articles had been gathered into piles. There were some articles of soldiers' equipment, too, canteens and cartridge belts, saddles and boots. One of the women had a yellow army neckerchief about her head, and an old man wore a soldier's coat. The bundles were being fastened on the backs of ponies, while in some cases big dogs were utilized as beasts of burden. Larger children had been assigned jobs, while smaller ones stayed well out of the way.

The pony herd had been moved nearer to camp. Guarded by boys, it waited close at hand for the moment of departure. Today there were new horses mingled with the Indian ponies, larger and with well-groomed coats, taken in yesterday's battle. They wore cavalry saddles, and on their flanks were burned the letters U.S.

The handful of old men present sat by themselves, talking eagerly. From time to time they paused to listen to the sound of steady gunfire in the distance. It came from the ridges beyond the Hunkpapa camp, and it was pleasing to the old men, for they smiled and nodded to each other. The only young warriors were the wounded, stretched out on travois and waiting to be fastened to the backs of horses.

Five boys, wearing fringed jackets and the high-laced moccasins of the Sioux, came quietly into camp. For a moment they stood hesitating, as though wondering what to do. No one appeared to notice their arrival. No one stopped work to offer the usual greeting to a stranger. Finally one of the boys spoke to a girl who was filling a basket with strips of dried meat.

"We seek the father of Fears No White Fanged Snake," he told her. "Is he here?"

The girl shook her head.

"The mother then?"

"She has gone, too. They left before daylight. They

said it was a long journey."

"Is there no member of the family here? Friends perhaps?"

"The brother, Walks at Night, fights against the soldiers on the ridge." The girl paused a moment to consider the question. "Ask of the boys who herd the ponies. They have more time to talk than I."

"She speaks with sense," approved one of the Sioux. "What would a girl know of Fears No White Fanged Snake? He would have no time for girls. We must talk with the boys."

"There are no burial lodges," said another, with a wondering glance around. "Did the Cheyenne lose no warriors in yesterday's battle?"

"You forget, Dog Chief," said his friend, "that the Cheyenne do not use burial lodges as we do. They hide their dead in caves."

"What about their possessions?" asked Dog Chief, as they started toward the pony herd. "Surely, Good Thunder, they don't keep them?"

"Of course not." Good Thunder scoffed at the idea. "The possessions of the dead are placed with the body in the cave. What would the Great Medicine think if a dead warrior came to him without his pipe or medicine bag or implements of warfare? He must take everything he owns with him to the other world."

The Cheyenne boys who were guarding the pony herd watched their arrival curiously. Obviously, it was strange to have visitors at a time when the camp was preparing to move. Then one of them, recognizing the moccasins of a Sioux, called out.

"How is the battle going? The one beyond the Hunkpapa camp?"

"The white soldiers are pinned upon the ridge," answered Good Thunder. "They are without water, and Crazy Horse says that given time we could get them all."

"Then why has the order come to move camp?"

"Sitting Bull has received news that more soldiers are on their way. He thinks it is better to leave now," explained Dog Chief. "Our warriors will leave the battle a few at a time to join their tribes. Your own Cheyenne should be coming soon, since you are in the lead. The Hunkpapas will stay until the last. When our people are so far ahead that the soldiers cannot catch up, the last of our warriors will leave off firing and join the march."

"You should have seen the battle yesterday," boasted Talking Crow. "The one across from the Cheyenne camp. Over two hundred soldiers came riding down the coulee to attack us. Not one remains alive."

"Our warriors were in it, too," said Dog Chief. "They told us of the battle. Some of them say the leader was the one called Long Hair, but no one is sure. They did not recognize him."

"Enough." Good Thunder frowned. "We are not here to speak of battles. Our errand is different. We five are those who yesterday rode with the Cheyenne, Fears No White Fanged Snake. Together we stirred up the dust cloud to distract the soldiers. Now we seek his friends."

There was an awkward moment of silence, then Bear Sits Down stepped forward.

"I knew him," he said. "We all knew him."

"Our grief mingles with yours at the loss of one so brave." Good Thunder spoke formally. "May the Great Medicine receive him with all honor."

"He did not have to ride with us," said Dog Chief. "We were the ones Gall asked. He volunteered."

"He liked to push into things." Talking Crow inched forward, and there was an edge to his tone that made the Sioux look at him in surprise. "He never waited to be asked."

"Sometimes that takes bravery." Good Thunder stared hard at Talking Crow, who lowered his eyes.

"I think he was brave," said Bear Sits Down thoughtfully. "He withstood a four-day vigil. None of the rest of us has done that. It is not usual to seek medicine before the sixteenth summer. Now that it is too late, I wish that I had known him better."

The Sioux boys nodded, saying nothing.

"But his vision wasn't a very good one," said Talking Crow. "It was only a rattlesnake. It didn't protect him yesterday, did it?"

"I think he wanted to be a medicine man, like his father," said Bear Sits Down. "The rattlesnake would have helped him then. He was always digging up bulbs and roots and bringing pieces of bark back to camp."

"Woman's work," said Talking Crow, but no one returned his half smile.

"He was wise to start on those things early," said Dog Chief severely, staring at Talking Crow. "Fears No White Fanged Snake was wise as well as brave. Had he lived, perhaps he would have become like our holy man, Sitting Bull."

"We come to pay our respects to his family," said Good Thunder. "Since the Hunkpapa will be the last camp to move in the day's march, there was time. Someone told us the father and mother are not here."

"They took the body of Fears No White Fanged Snake away," said Bear Sits Down. "White Buffalo said he knew of a cave, high in the rocks, where no one would find it. He said the cave was guarded by Fears No White Fanged Snake's secret helpers. Only in the Moon of Drying Grasses can he reach it safely."

"They took all of his things, his best beaded shirt and moccasins, his flute, his bow, and his medicine bag and left before it was light," said Talking Crow eagerly. He seemed to be trying to undo the impression he had made on the Sioux. "They know the way we are going, but White Buffalo said it would be three suns before they could catch up. The cave must be a long way off."

"When he returns, tell White Buffalo that the friends of his son, Fears No White Fanged Snake, mourn for him," said Good Thunder. "Say that we will never forget him, and may his secret helpers guard him well."

The dream ended, and Jamie stared into darkness. He was wide awake, and his head was pounding.

These dreams, all connected as though they were telling a story, were not like any others he had ever had. The details of each one remained vividly in his mind. They didn't fade, the way dreams usually did.

White Fang had given him a good many of the facts, he realized, and the books he read had supplied a lot of the details, but he was sure there was more to it than that. The dreams had a purpose.

Suddenly, he knew what it was. He was sure that the body of Fears No White Fanged Snake lay in the rattlesnake cave, high in the Indian rocks. The medicine bag, hidden in the bureau drawer, belonged to him. And he wanted Jamie to return it to him.

Chapter Sixteen

To Jamie's delight, Charley brought Horse with him when he came to work the next morning. He excused himself long enough to run to his room and tuck the medicine bag into his shirt. Then he and Horse saddled Old Sal and rode to the rocks. As soon as they arrived, he produced the bag.

"So that's it," said Horse, turning it over in his hands. "It looks a lot like Grandfather's, but I don't think it's Cheyenne. I asked around as much as I dared, but nobody admits to losing one."

"They didn't lose it," Jamie told him positively. "It fell out of the rattlesnake cave up there in the rocks."

"Since when did rattlesnakes have medicine bags?" scoffed Horse. Then his expression changed. "You mean somebody's buried up there? With all those snakes crawling around?"

"They're not up there three months out of the year. He could have been buried then," Jamie reminded him. "I found it right below the entrance. It was hanging on the rocks. That was the day after the snakes left. Maybe one of them jostled it loose from wherever it was."

"It looks pretty old." Horse fingered the bag thoughtfully. "Maybe older than Grandfather's. And the Cheyenne did bury people in caves. But they filled up the entrance with rocks so nobody would know."

"Here they wouldn't have to," Jamie pointed out. "The rattlesnakes would keep people away. They always come back to the same cave to hibernate."

"I don't know." Horse squinted at the hole high in the cliff. "It would be a hard place to get to."

"Maybe the cliff has changed. It's been over a hundred years since the Battle of the Little Big Horn. Rocks wear away. Maybe it was easier to get to then."

"What makes you think whoever it is was buried then?" asked Horse.

"Because I think it's your grandfather's brother, Round Stone."

"Round Stone? The kid that was killed riding with the Sioux?" Evidently Horse was familiar with the story. He stared at Jamie, then he began to grin. "Oh, come on. I know Grandfather says somebody's buried around here, but even he doesn't claim it's Round Stone."

"How about the thing he said when he got sick?" said Jamie stubbornly. "That a member of his family was angry. Well, whoever's up there lost his medicine bag when it fell out of the cave, didn't he? And that would certainly make him pretty mad."

For just a second Horse's eyes shifted uneasily. Then he was himself again.

"Grandfather's mind was wandering," he insisted. "The doctor said so."

Jamie took a deep breath. Even though it might cost him a friend, he would have to tell Horse about the dreams. After that the Cheyenne might decide that Jamie was odd and someone to be avoided. But he had to take the chance.

He began at the beginning and told Horse all about them—about Round Stone, who became Fears No White Fanged Snake, and about Bear Sits Down and Talking Crow. He told about the battle and its aftermath, when the five Sioux boys came to the camp and found that the body had been carried away for burial in a cave where his secret helpers, the rattlesnakes, would stand guard.

"Hey," said Horse admiringly, when he finished. "That's just like a movie. A lot of it I'd heard from Grandfather, but the way you tell it is better. You fill in the empty spots. Sure you didn't make it up?"

"I don't think so," Jamie told him honestly. "I dreamed it."

"The old medicine men used to see things in their visions. I guess they were a little like dreams," said

Horse, after a moment. "Grandfather says he's had a few, and his father had them all the time. People laugh at them now, but I never heard anybody laugh at Sitting Bull's vision of soldiers riding into camp the way they did."

Jamie looked at him gratefully. Horse didn't think he was peculiar.

"You're not a medicine man, and I never heard of a white man having a vision, but you did have a Cheyenne medicine bag," continued Horse carefully. "Maybe that helped it along. And there could be somebody buried up there."

"I think it's Round Stone, Fears No White Fanged Snake," insisted Jamie. "And when his medicine bag dropped out and I found it, he sent me those dreams."

"Come on, Jim," said Horse uncomfortably. "Why would he pick on you? If somebody like Grandfather found it, there'd be some sense to it. But not you."

"He picked on me because Fears No White Fanged Snake and I are an awful lot alike," said Jamie slowly. "You remember I told you how nobody liked him because he was always collecting bulbs and flowers and things? At home the kids all think I'm nuts because I used to carry books around."

"What did you do that for?" asked Horse curiously.

"To read. To find out things I didn't know," explained Jamie. "I don't have any friends at home. You're the first friend I ever had, Horse. I'm like Fears No White Fanged Snake. He didn't have any friends either till he met those Sioux boys."

"You're kidding," objected Horse. "You've got lots of friends."

"No, I haven't. And I think that's why Fears No White Fanged Snake picked me to find the bag. Because we're so much alike. If I were buried in that cave, I'd pick somebody as near like me as possible to return something that was important to me."

"Return it?" Horse stared at him in amazement. "You're not thinking of trying to put it back?"

"I have to," Jamie told him.

"I don't see how you can," said Horse practically. "Even if you managed to crawl up there, you couldn't make those last ten feet. They're just straight up and down."

"There must be a way," insisted Jamie. "White Buffalo did it when he put his son's body in the cave."

"White Buffalo?" This time there was definite uneasiness in Horse's eyes. "Where'd you hear that name? Grandfather wouldn't have said it aloud."

"It was in the dream."

"You must have heard it somewhere," said Horse. "He was Grandfather's father. I wouldn't know his name but he was kind of famous. He had a sign or something just before the battle that the soldiers would come that day. Some of our people still talk about him. It makes Grandfather pretty mad when they do." He got up hastily and thrust the medicine bag into Jamie's hands.

"Let's get out of here," he said. "This is a creepy place."

They left the Indian rocks and rode out into the sunshine. Jamie let Sal choose her own way. They passed the fenced fields, heading east. He could feel the warmth of Horse's body through his cotton shirt, but they did not speak. Now that he had made a full confession, Jamie was beginning to have second thoughts. He probably should have kept the whole thing to himself.

When they reached the upper limits of the ranch, Sal stopped. This area had not yet been cleared. There were bushes and straggling trees, under which the protected grass still retained a vestige of green. Sal lowered her head and began to nibble.

"Get down," ordered Horse. "And watch for snakes before you pick a spot to sit. We need to talk some more."

Jamie swung from the saddle. He was doing it very well by now. It didn't take several tries before he could get on and off a horse.

"I guess it was just chance that made you dream up the name of White Buffalo." Horse came immediately to the point. "Lots of medicine men used it. The white buffalo was supposed to be sacred. There weren't very many of them, and whenever one was killed the hide and horns were always given to the medicine man."

"Maybe I read it somewhere," agreed Jamie meekly. Of course, such a thing was possible. The name could have been stored in his mind for a long time.

"And there could be somebody buried in that cave," continued Horse. "Maybe it is Round Stone. I don't know whether his real name was Fears No White Fanged Snake, though."

Jamie sat very still. He didn't want to interrupt. Horse seemed to be thinking out loud.

"Maybe Grandfather knew, or maybe he just guessed. The old-timers knew a lot of things that we don't know anymore. It's like him saying that he's going to die. My mother says he will, too. Even though the doctor says Grandfather's fine, she says if he wants to die he can make it happen."

Jamie remembered that Uncle Bill had claimed no one could will himself to die, but he didn't think he should say so. Horse was too serious.

"Old people like Grandfather believe in visions, but I'm not so sure. I've had a lot of screwy dreams, but they didn't make sense."

"But these did," Jamie told him. "It was just like somebody was trying to explain something to me."

"It's spooky all right," agreed Horse uneasily. "They used to say that a dead spirit could put a curse —of course, I don't believe that junk, but just in case, I don't think we ought to take a chance."

"You mean you're going to help me?"

"You found the bag and you had the visions, but you're not a Cheyenne," said Horse, "I am, and if there is a guy in that cave and he is a Cheyenne, then

I'm mixed up in it too."

"Do you know how to get up the last ten feet?"

"I've got an idea," said Horse slowly. "It wouldn't be the way White Buffalo—if it *was* White Buffalo—did it, but it might work. Pete Longtree's brother used to work up in the Tetons as a guide. He's got some of the equipment they used to climb mountains. It's stored out in their barn. There's a rope, with a metal hook on one end, that you can throw over a ledge and pull yourself up. If we can toss it into the cave, maybe it will hold."

"Then we can get up there and return the bag," cried Jamie. He felt happy and excited. Horse was going to help! "When can we do it?" he demanded.

"Well," Horse scratched his head thoughtfully. "I'll go over to Pete's tonight and borrow the rope. But I don't know when my father will let me off from work again. Charley had to do a lot of talking before he let me come today."

"Come as soon as you can," begged Jamie. "Fears No White Fanged Snake really wants his medicine bag back."

Chapter Seventeen

SEVERAL DAYS WENT BY WITH NO WORD FROM HORSE.
Jamie inquired every morning, but Charley always
said their father was keeping him busy on the farm.

Then one day Charley arrived for work and the
usual smile was missing from his face. He looked
tired, as though he had been up all night.

"I'm fine," he explained in answer to Aunt Nora's
question about his health. "It's Grandfather. The
doctor says he probably won't last through the day."

"Why don't you go home, Charley?" suggested
Uncle Bill. "Take the day off."

"It's better for me to work," said Charley. "There's
nothing I can do there. He's got the whole family
around him, and a lot of friends have come in.
There's so many people now that I'm only in the
way."

"I'll bake something for you to take home," said Aunt Nora. "With extra people to feed, it will come in handy."

Jamie sat on at the breakfast table after the men had gone. Horse said that the old Cheyenne could actually will themselves to die. Was it about to happen to White Fang?

Dick came back into the kitchen, letting the screen door bang behind him.

"I've got to drive in to Lame Deer," he said. "Dad's low on oil. Anything you need, Mom?"

"I shopped Saturday," she told him. "Why didn't your father send Charley? It's only a mile out of the way to the Whites' place, and he could have checked on his grandfather."

"Maybe he didn't want to go." Dick opened the freezer, reaching for an ice-cream bar. He whistled as he bent to inspect the contents. "I didn't know you had all this stuff. There's cakes and pies and bread and all kind of frozen stuff. How come, when I'm looking for something to eat, you never said anything about all this?"

"It wouldn't have lasted long if you'd known about it." She pushed him out of the way and looked inside the freezer herself. "I believe I'll send the Whites one of these cakes instead of baking another," she said thoughtfully. "It will be thawed by the time it gets there."

"Maybe Dick could take it now," suggested Jamie. "I'll go with him, if he'll let me." This could be his chance to speak with Horse, to find out how he was getting along with their plans.

"Sure you can go," said Dick. "But I don't know about dropping off a cake. Let Charley take it tonight."

"I'll take it in," offered Jamie quickly. "You can just sit in the car."

Aunt Nora agreed that the Whites could probably use the cake early, and besides if there was any news Charley would want to hear as soon as possible. Dick grumbled a little but finally consented to stop, and he and Jamie went outside and got in the jeep.

The farms on the Cheyenne reservation were smaller than Uncle Bill's and not so well kept up. Many of the buildings needed paint and some of the fences looked as though they could stand repairs. But the crops looked healthy and so did the small herds grazing in the pastures.

Dick chattered away and Jamie answered absently, hardly aware of what he was saying. But when Dick announced they were approaching Frank White's land, he looked around with interest. The fences here were in good condition, and the stalks of grain poking through the wire were heavy-headed.

"It's Charley's doing," explained Dick. "He's a good farmer, and what he learns at the University he uses. After he gets through working for us, he probably comes home and puts in another four hours every day."

Charley's influence had not extended to the farmhouse, for like most of the others its paint was almost worn away. But it had a new roof, and the surrounding yard was free of litter.

A number of children left off playing as the jeep bounced up to the back door. A dog began to bark and two white geese hissed angrily. Clutching the cellophane-wrapped cake, Jamie climbed to the ground, his eyes searching for his friend. There were several empty cars standing near the steps, but there was no sign of all the visitors Charley had mentioned.

"Where's Horse?" he asked the children.

They were all very young and most of them only stared without speaking, but one boy replied shyly that Horse was in the barn, then volunteered to get him.

"White Fang's still alive anyway," observed Dick from the jeep.

"How do you know?" asked Jamie curiously.

"No sounds of mourning. Everybody's probably sitting in there, waiting."

The back door opened, and a man stepped out on the porch.

"That's Frank White," said Dick in a low voice. "Go give him the cake."

Jamie walked over to the porch. Frank White was broad-shouldered like Horse, but his angular face was thin, like Charley's. He did not smile, nor did he offer any greeting.

"Good morning," said Jamie bravely. "I'm Jim

Steele. I'm a friend of your sons. My aunt, Mrs. Bennett, sent this cake. Charley said you had a lot of guests, and she thought you could use it."

"She is a good woman." The hardened brown hands moved carefully to accept the present. "Tell her thank you."

"How is Mr. White Fang? Is he any better?"

"No change," said Frank White.

Horse came hurrying from the barn. He did not call out from a distance but waited until he was close before he spoke.

"Hello, Jim. You met my father?"

"We met," said Frank White.

"Can you stay awhile?" asked Horse eagerly.

"I wish I could. But I don't think I should, not with your grandfather so sick. Besides, you probably have work to do."

"I've done it. Everything you told me, Pop. Maybe I could ride back with Jim and Dick and drive home with Charley. You said I was to keep out of the way today."

"We'd like to have him," said Jamie quickly. "Please let him come. Uncle Bill will probably send Charley home early."

"Then go." Frank White turned and went back into the house.

Dick was agreeable to bringing Horse home with them. He didn't even mind waiting an extra few minutes while Horse ran to fetch something from the barn. It was large and bulky and filled a burlap potato sack.

"What you got there?" he asked curiously, when Horse threw the sack in behind.

"Oh, it's a kind of game," said Horse evasively. "Jim and I thought we'd try it out."

As soon as they returned to the ranch, Jamie hurried to get his own equipment. He had everything collected in one place. Besides the medicine bag, which was to be returned to the cave, he had gloves to avoid rope burns, rubber-soled tennis shoes that would cling to the rocks, and a flashlight. They got Old Sal from the corral, tied the burlap bag onto the saddle, and started for the rocks.

"What's that?" asked Horse curiously, pointing to the one sack that hadn't been explained to him.

"It's lunch," said Jamie. "I don't want to go home at noon, so I told Aunt Nora we wanted to have a picnic."

"I could eat something now," said Horse pointedly, but Jamie pretended not to hear.

When they arrived at the rocks, Horse removed the rope from the burlap sack. On one end was a long spiked hook which could be secured around ledges or slid into crevices. Jamie knew it had a special name, but he couldn't remember what it was.

"The quickest way is to climb straight up," said Horse thoughtfully. "But it looks awful steep. I don't know if we could get a toehold."

"When the snakes came down, they crawled at an

angle. Maybe they've worn ruts in the rocks. Come on and I'll show you," offered Jamie.

He led the way to the spot where the snakes had dropped to the ground. Horse threw the rope and managed to find a crevice that held the hook. Then he shinnied up and for a moment clung there, his eyes inspecting the surface.

Jamie watched him enviously. He would never have been able to do this without Horse's help. He couldn't throw a rope, and he didn't think he could climb one either.

"That won't work," said Horse, sliding back down. "Maybe a snake can hang on there, but I can't. Let's try another spot. What we need are ledges to step on."

For some time they kept at it. Horse threw the rope and secured the hook in several different places, then like a monkey shinned up to inspect the cliff. Each time he had to report failure. It was impossible.

Jamie grew more and more depressed. He stared up at the black hole, which marked the entrance to the cave, and thought about Fears No White Fanged Snake waiting for the return of his medicine bag.

"I don't know where else to try," Horse admitted finally. "Anyway, I've got to get my breath back. That takes a lot of wind."

"Let's eat lunch," suggested Jamie. He felt guilty that Horse had done all the work, while he only stood by watching.

"There has to be a way up there," he said as they

ate Aunt Nora's sandwiches and cookies. "How could White Buffalo have carried Fears No White Fanged Snake's body up there if there wasn't?"

"We aren't sure this is the cave," pointed out Horse. "And even if it is, you said yourself it could have changed."

"I wonder, do you suppose we could climb up the other side and then slide down? Is the rope long enough to reach?"

"It would reach all right." Horse squinted at the dark hole high in the cliff. "It might be pretty dangerous, but I guess I could try."

"No," said Jamie quickly. "I've got to do it. I found the medicine bag, and I have to be the one who puts it back."

"Have you ever climbed a rope?"

"No." Jamie's face grew red. "But you could tie it around me and let me down, couldn't you? It would be a lot safer than having you swing out there on the rope without anything to hold you."

"I suppose so." Horse fished in the lunch sack for another cookie. "It would take a lot of nerve, though."

When they finished eating, they went around to inspect the outer side of the cliff. After a few moments, Horse declared that this would be a cinch, but they would have to watch for rattlesnakes. It was closer to water, and the snakes might be coiled under protecting ledges of rocks. There was no trail leading to the top, but the slope was gradual and broken by jutting boulders. He led the way, carrying the rope, and Jamie followed, trying to place his feet where Horse had put his, his ears strained for the warning sound of a rattle.

The ascent took a long time. Horse carefully tried each foothold, making sure that the rock would not crumble beneath him, and several times they had to stop to rest. The sun beat down, and their shirts were drenched with perspiration. Horse took his off and left it on a boulder. Once Jamie glanced at his watch and saw that it was after two. Ho hoped they could complete their mission and get back down before Charley was ready to go home and came looking for them.

At last they reached the top. Fortunately, the two sides did not come to a peak but formed a ledge several feet across. Horse lay down on his back, panting, and Jamie did the same. He felt strange, and it was a feeling he had never know before. Part of it was fear for the thing he meant to do, but part was excitement. Of all the people in the world, the spirit of Fears No White Fanged Snake had chosen him to fulfill a mission, and he was going to do it.

After a while Horse sat up.

"We better get started," he said. "Sure you don't want me to do it?"

"No," Jamie assured him positively. "You stay here and pull me up after I've left the medicine bag."

"OK." Horse didn't argue. He tied one end of the rope securely around Jamie's waist and jammed the hook over the side of the ledge they had just climbed. "That's just a double precaution," he said.

"What do I do?" Jamie tried to make his voice fearless. "Jump?"

"Don't be a kook!" Horse glared at him, and Jamie knew that he was trying to hide his concern. "You just ease yourself off. Try to get handholds on the cliff as you go down. You may not be able to, but it will slow you down some. I'll hold the rope and let it out until you get there."

Jamie nodded. He sat on the edge above the cave, then turned himself so he was facing the cliff. Horse held the rope, easing it slowly as he went down the side, clutching and clawing to find crevices that were not there.

It was happening so fast that he had no time to think, and when the fingers of one hand closed around a rough edge of rock, he clutched it automatically. His descent was halted, and from above he heard Horse calling anxiously.

"That's the end of the rope. Are you far enough down to see in?"

Not until then did he realize that he had reached the cave. The rough rock in his hand was the side of the opening. Unfortunately the rope had been too short to let him reach the floor, and he was hanging suspended midway at the entrance.

"Are you OK?" called Horse again. "Can you see anything?"

"I'm OK." Jamie tried to swallow his disappointment. After all this, he was not going to be able to go inside the cave. He could only look in, and if there was a tunnel that curved deeply into the rock, he wouldn't be able to see very much.

He tried to push himself around to get a better view, but the taut rope about his waist refused to move. He had to stay where he was, suspended in the air. Below him, at the entrance was a wide ledge. It was invisible from the ground, and was probably used by the rattlesnakes for sunning themselves in the early days of spring. If only the rope had been a few feet longer, he could have stood on that. But it wasn't, and there was no use thinking about it.

He reached into his back pocket and carefully withdrew the flashlight, thinking how lucky it was he had remembered to bring it. The entrance was not large and let in little light.

It was awkward using a flashlight with one hand and grasping the edge of the cave with the other. If he were truly brave, he told himself, he would let go. But he couldn't make himself do it. The rope was secure, but he felt better with that edge of rock in his hand.

The beam of light circled a small rocky room. It was not nearly large enough to accommodate all the snakes he had seen descending the cliff, so it had to open into a second room. Yes, there it was. The opening was in the rear in the middle of the wall. He had to stretch his neck and peer around the edge before he could see it. Then his hand began to shake, and the light bobbed up and down.

Lying against the wall next to him was a long, cigar-shaped bundle. It was wrapped in something dark, perhaps a blanket or a skin of some kind. Piled over the top was an assortment of articles. Jamie saw a bowl and what could have been a quiver filled with arrows. He had no time to distinguish anything else, for his hand had become too weak to hold the flashlight. It dropped, bouncing off the ledge and falling to the ground below.

"Hey, what happened?" called Horse in alarm.

"I dropped the flashlight." He heard his own voice come out in a strange, echoing croak and was ashamed. He had come here expecting to find a dead warrior, and now that it had happened he was acting like a baby.

"Too bad," commiserated Horse. "I better pull you back up. You can't see without it."

"Just a minute." Quickly he fumbled in his shirt for the medicine bag. Then leaning out as far as he dared, he tossed it into the darkness of the cave. "OK," he called. "Pull away."

Horse was red-faced and gasping by the time Jamie was safely on the ledge.

"I ought to have my head examined for letting you do that," he said. "It was a crazy thing for us to do."

"No, it wasn't," insisted Jamie. "Nobody's hurt. The only damage is to my watch. I broke the crystal when I tossed the medicine bag inside the cave. But

I can always get a new crystal."

"Did you see anything?"

"There's a dead Indian in there all right. He's all wrapped up in robes, and there's a lot of stuff stacked around him. Of course," he admitted honestly, "it might not be Fears No White Fanged Snake."

"I'm glad I didn't have to see him," said Horse. "I'd have backed out of this a long time ago except I was afraid you'd think I was chicken."

"I'd never think that, Horse," Jamie told him seriously. "I wish I could be like you."

"Aw, cut it out." Horse was embarrassed. He turned and began picking his way down the rocks. When he arrived at a sizable ledge, he stopped.

"You got guts," he said gruffly. "Don't let anybody tell you different."

Jamie felt warm and happy inside. Horse admired him. He was a real friend. Of course, they could never tell anyone what they had done. Their families would be upset at the chance they had taken—Mother especially. She must never find out that her son had dangled by a rope from a hundred foot cliff. Maybe, though, a long time from now he might tell his father. Jamie had received several letters from Dad since the one he had written about the rodeo, and they had all been addressed to "Jim."

Charley was just driving up when they rounded the spur of rocks.

"You're a fine one," he said, eyeing the coil of rope over Horse's arm. "Playing at mountain climbing while Grandfather is home dying."

"I'm sorry," said Horse contritely. "But there wasn't anything I could do. Did you want me to sit with the old people and just wait?"

"No," said his brother, relenting a little. "I guess that wouldn't have done much good."

Nobody expected Charley to show up for work the next day, but he arrived. Moreover, he was smiling widely.

"Grandfather's better," he told them. "Yesterday afternoon he turned over in bed and announced that he was hungry. After he'd swallowed some soup, he got up and said he wasn't ready to die just yet."

"You see," said Uncle Bill. "A man can't will himself to die. It's just like I told you."

"For goodness' sakes!" Aunt Nora shook her head in amazement. "Did he give any reason for changing his mind?"

"Just that the member of the family who had been angry, wasn't anymore," said Charley grinning. "Which is silly, because no one was angry in the first place."

"What time did this happen?" asked Jamie in a small voice.

"Oh, a couple of hours before I got home. Middle of the afternoon. Around three o'clock, I suppose," said Charley. "Why?"

"I just wondered," said Jamie.

He remembered that it had been just three o'clock

when he had broken the crystal on his watch by toss-
ing the medicine bag into the darkness of Rattlesnake
Cave.

EVELYN SIBLEY LAMPMAN was born in Dallas, Oregon, which is a small town in Willamette Valley, mecca of the covered wagon pioneers. Her great-grandparents made that trip themselves. Her father was a lawyer which, in a small town, meant he served various terms as mayor, district attorney, and county judge. He was also a good storyteller and some of Evelyn's happiest recollections are of sitting around the fireplace, cracking walnuts (including one for the cat, who was fond of them), and taking turns reading aloud. Then her father would tell her stories, often of the early settlers of the Willamette Valley and of the Indians on the reservation twenty miles away. Her father was very sympathetic with the Indians and their problems, a rare thing in those days, and when they came to town they always stopped by to see him. Through his stories, her father was able to make many of these settlers and Indians, whom Evelyn never saw, very real to her.

After completing her school locally, Evelyn went on to Oregon State and was graduated from there, with a degree in Education. She had no intention of teaching, however, and took a job in a Portland radio station as a continuity writer. In addition, she gave a daily cooking talk over the air, though she was not much of a cook. Finally, she says, her recipes got so bad that her program was taken off the air!

Marriage followed and two daughters, which occupied Evelyn full time. With her husband's death eight years later, she went back to radio work as continuity chief, which led to her appointment as Educational Director of special programs that were being broadcast into the classrooms of the Portland Public Schools. She wrote all the programs herself. Her first book for children was published in 1948 and, in time, she was able to give up her radio work and concentrate entirely on her books, as she has done ever since.

Until the end of 1972, Mrs. Lampman lived in the same house she and her husband had bought thirty years ago. It was big and old and drafty, with dark paneling and high ceilings. There were nine rooms and a huge yard, gradually growing into a jungle— and Evelyn loved it. Prodded by friends and family, she finally sold it and moved to a new house in an apple orchard on the outskirts of Portland, which, she says, "in time will begin to feel like home."

Among her many published books are *Go Up The Road*, *Cayuse Courage*, and *The Year Of Small Shadow*.